THE SUNDOG SEASON

Ottawa
May 25/05

Rose

THE SUNDOG SEASON

a novel by

John Geddes

*with deep
affection,

John*

TURNSTONE PRESS

Turnstone Press
Artspace Building
607-100 Arthur Street
Winnipeg, MB
R3B 1H3 Canada
www.TurnstonePress.com

Turnstone Press gratefully acknowledges the assistance of The Canada
Council for the Arts, the Manitoba Arts Council, the Government of
Canada through the Book Publishing Industry Development Program and
the Government of Manitoba through the Department of Culture,
Heritage and Tourism, Arts Branch, for our publishing activities.

 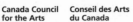

Cover design: Tétro Design
Interior design: Sharon Caseburg
Printed and bound in Canada by Kromar Printing Ltd. for Turnstone Press.

Library and Archives Canada Cataloguing in Publication

Geddes, John, 1961-
   The sundog season / John Geddes.

ISBN 0-88801-306-X

   I. Title.

PS8613.E44S86 2005   C813'.6   C2005-900773-7

To Giovanna

Thanks to Rose Moss for her expert guidance and to the Nieman Fellows who participated in her writing group at Harvard in 2002-2003 for their many insightful suggestions.

THE SUNDOG SEASON

BEFORE/

When I was five years old I wished for the death of another boy, prayed for it, and it happened. This was in the early spring after a winter that was very cold, even by the standards of the place where I grew up. These details come back to me even though I am really trying to remember a different stretch of my childhood, events that happened eight years later. But I'll get to that.

My family moved to the little mining town of West Spirit Lake in the summer before I entered kindergarten. We came from a suburb where I played on lawns to a trailer park in the bush. I preferred the new place from the start. My father was a pharmacist, and he was lured north by the chance to buy the town's drugstore and be his own boss. I didn't realize it at the start, of course, but this put us in a distinct category in the community, along with the teachers, the town clerk, the two doctors, and the one dentist. Practically everybody else worked in the mine.

The trailer park was a mile from the edge of town. In old snapshots I see how bleak it must have been for my mother. The single-width trailers perch on grey, crushed rock. There is no grass. The sign of a long-term occupant is a closed-in porch of unpainted plywood built around the door, or a concrete slab patio with a barbecue. But we didn't bother with anything like that; our real house was being built for us in town on a nice lot overlooking the lake. Mom would have to make do for only a year.

That can be a long time, though. The way I remember that summer, it's as if I had unlimited opportunity to explore the beaver swamp that marked one end of the trailer park. My older sister would come with me, since there was no one else around to play with. But we soon discovered signs that there must have been children in some of the trailers before us. Our most important find was what remained of a tree house, built of scrap lumber in a triangle between three skinny poplars. When we first climbed the rotting rungs nailed into one tree trunk, we found some rusty pots and pans up there. These relics we examined closely.

"Kids from before played house in this fort," Katie told me. "This was a girls' place."

I accepted her interpretation of the evidence. Katie and I were never so much together or so happy in each other's company as we were then. I suppose it was by necessity. Not so many years later, she would become a mystery to me, a story, maybe a sad one, which I could never quite read to a satisfying conclusion. But at the end of that August, we were together, wearing the same wounds on our shins and elbows, the day-old scrapes scabbed over dark red and the month-old ones pale as larvae. We were tanned the same tawny shade.

"The scouting party returns," my father would say when we came in the door. "How's hunting in these parts?"

The start of school changed everything. An old yellow bus looped around town to pick up children who lived too far to walk. Katie and I were the only public school kids from the trailer park, although four high school students also waited with us at the bus stop—three boys who swore and a wordless girl with a green Export A pack peeking out of the breast pocket of her jean jacket.

4

The bus made two other stops. First was Tecumseh Drive, a cluster of a dozen three-room houses where the Indians lived, a little beyond the parking lot shared by the hockey arena and the curling rink. Then came Babcock's Corners, a crossroads where the owner of the town's only gas station had thrown up six cottages along a riverbank, thinking he would rent them in the summer to sport fishermen. Instead, Mr. Babcock ended up year-round landlord to a mixed bag of tenants—the family of a miner who was fired for being too drunk too often underground and lost his company house, and a hunting guide who made a little money in the warm months but went on pogey every winter, and some others.

In all, there couldn't have been more than fifteen kids let off that bus every morning by the chain-link fence of West Spirit Lake Public School.

I spent the first week or two of school trying to stay within a few yards of Katie. There is a photograph of us, a favourite of my mother's, dressed up and clinging to our lunch boxes. It must have been our first day, but already Katie looks like she is edging away from me. At eight, she is as poised as a child catalogue model for back-to-school fashions. Her hair, which would go straight, is still wavy. In the schoolyard, she was the most expert skipper anyone had seen, never stumbling, her voice touching each rhyming word precisely, like notes from a xylophone. I wonder if she sings anymore, or still plays the piano much.

Cowboy Joe
From Mexico
Hands up
Stick 'em up
Drop your guns
And pick 'em up

I don't know exactly when I first heard the words *trailer failer*. I think it was from a rival of Katie's, maybe the girl who had been the best skipper before we showed up, who tried it out one recess. The words meant nothing to me at first, but Katie got the sense of them, recognizing an epithet of old meaning in this schoolyard.

"But we're not trailer failers. Our house is being built beside Dr. Rooney's," she said with a wave in the direction of the waterfront.

Indeed, from the school's gravel playground, which shared the plateau of the town with the mine itself, we could look down to the street along the lakeshore where the hole for our basement had been dug in the last vacant lot. The cement was already being poured.

So Katie was left alone. But after a while, it became clear that she was one thing and I was another. She soon tired of my shadowing her and her new friends. The best I could do before the morning bell or during recess was to keep my eye on her from a distance. The sandbox was a good place to watch from. Other five-year-olds played there with me until, as the weeks passed, the sand was too cold for bare hands. Finally, only I persisted.

A boy alone is a target. One October day I looked up from the sand to see a fat kid with black hair looking down at me. This was Alvin Pierkowski, who was only a year older than me, but much bigger.

"Trailer failer."

"But we're not ..."

"Trailer failer."

And he stepped onto my hand where it was splayed on the cold sand and twisted hard with the rubber heel of his black canvas running shoe.

That was as badly as I had ever been hurt intentionally by anyone. From then on, some small pain was a daily expectation. After the snow fell in early November, it worsened. Often he came for me the minute I got off the bus. Sometimes I ran, and I was faster than Alvin, but eventually he would corner me against the fence. Then I would grip the chain links until the sheer weight of him pulled my hands loose and he had me down in the snow.

Sometimes a teacher on duty would intervene.

"Alvin, no giving snow faces."

But I got a lot of them. Katie saw. She forbade me to tell our parents.

"Just wait until we're in our house, then it'll all be over. If you tell Mom now and she comes to school, we'll be trailer failers for the rest of our lives."

My enemy never hurt me much. My most vivid memory is not of injury, but of my own mittens pressed against my face for protection as he tried to pry them away, which he always succeeded in doing. The mittens were brown woollen ones with a blue or red stripe at the cuff, knitted by my faraway grandmother and mailed as presents. Grandma used a type of oily wool that kept the heat in even when sopping wet, and whenever I catch a whiff of something barnyardy, the smell of them comes back to me.

I started asking for a bath every night, which my parents allowed. In the hot tub I would think about my enemy. There was only one bathroom in the trailer, of course, so most evenings Katie would come to the door at some point and demand that I get out. But I would block out her voice and stay in until my hands were deeply wrinkled.

It was while looking at my pink fingers after a bath one night that I started thinking about Alvin Pierkowski's death. This must have been in January, because I know we had recently been to church, and our family attended only at Christmas and Easter. I put my hands together and contemplated asking God to kill my enemy.

The thought was so unexpected that I forced it quickly from my mind, but then I brought my hands together again. To fool myself, I pretended that this was to perform the little rhyme about the church and the steeple. I'm sure Katie, who loved this sort of thing, must have taught me.

Here is the church,
And here is the steeple,
Open the doors,
And see all the people.

I did it once the way it is supposed to be done. Then I started again.

I folded my hands together with the fingers inward against the palms.

Here is the church.

I raised my index fingers and touched their tips together.

And here is the steeple.

Now, however, I stopped, never completing the verse. I kept the people inside, wiggling them a little. I opened the doors, my thumbs, slightly, to look at them. They would pray along with me. God, kill Alvin Pierkowski. I'm not sure if I whispered these words or just thought them. It doesn't matter.

How many times I prayed this way, I can't say. Almost every day. More often than my enemy attacked me, I would guess, since my relentless hate did not take Saturdays and Sundays off.

Winters are long in the country north of Lake Superior, and West Spirit Lake is about as far north as one can travel without resorting to a float plane or a canoe. The sub-zero weather usually persists until well into March. When spring comes in April, the general relief in a northern town can feel like a muscle spasm that suddenly relaxes, a discomfort borne so long it is forgotten until it goes away.

Like everyone else, I was happier. Alvin let up a little. Without snow and ice as weapons, he may have run out of ideas for how to torment me. Maybe my weak resistance was beginning to be dull even to a six-year-old bully. By this time, though, the praying had become a habit for me.

The ice in West Spirit Lake stayed long after the snow had shrunk back to slushy patches in shady places. That winter had been so cold that the lake ice was as thick as six feet. Even after three weeks of warm weather, with May around the corner, it still looked black and solid. Then a hard rain fell on a Sunday, followed by a warm, windy Monday morning, the perfect combination for taking the ice out.

This was the first time I saw breakup. From our schoolyard, we little kids watched as teenaged boys, skipping their high school classes, jumped from one mattress-sized iceberg to another. Sometimes one would slip and soak a boot, but that didn't seem to bother them. The air was warm enough to bear it. I could make out the foursome from our trailer park, the three boys running and jumping and balancing and skidding on the ice floes, the girl smoking a cigarette on shore, watching them without betraying much interest.

That evening at dinner, I told my mother and father about the fun of playing on the breaking ice. They warned me sternly against it, and even briefly discussed walking over to knock on the doors of some of the trailer park teenagers to inform their parents about the danger. Katie pleaded with them not to embarrass us; she insisted I was making up the part about recognizing some of the daredevils on the ice. So they relented, but warned us again not to go near the shoreline. My father alluded to Dr. Rooney's having told him about past tragedies at breakup time.

Now I probe my memory and it fails me. I have a vivid image of Alvin Pierkowski going down into the black water in a fissure between blocks of thick, jagged ice. Of course I didn't witness this scene. But did I imagine it, conjure it up, before it happened, or only after the boy was drowned?

It could be that later on that same evening, when our family discussed the dangers of playing on the rotting ice at dinner, I might have made my prayer more specific. Not just death, but the manner of death. Clear instructions for the first time: part the ice and swallow up my enemy.

Or, more likely, I visualized it after it all came to pass.

For Alvin did not come to school on Tuesday. Nor did his two sisters. By that afternoon the whole town knew why. He had fallen into frigid water just a few yards offshore. Two other boys had run for help, but he was long dead by the time a police officer used a chainsaw to cut through the ice, which had closed again over the place where he had gone in, to retrieve his body.

I did not speak for two days. That much is family lore. I did not cry, but awoke screaming and sweaty in the middle of the second night. My parents took my reaction for sensitivity, the sign of a good boyish heart, full of feeling. Only Katie guessed it was something more. When my father said we should visit the Pierkowskis after the funeral, I pleaded to stay home, but he said nonsense, we had been "little friends," and it would do Alvin's poor mother good to see how badly her son would be missed by his playmates.

When we arrived, their small house was full of people. Katie strode resolutely over to Alvin's sisters and began a solemn conversation. She always knew how to handle herself on an occasion. I clung to my parents as they made their way through the crowded kitchen to the living room where Mr. and Mrs. Pierkowski were sitting three feet apart on the couch behind a coffee table covered with cookies and cakes. She looked up; he kept his face down.

My father said, "Mrs. Pierkowski, we haven't met, I'm the new pharmacist."

"We just wanted to say how sorry we are," said my mother. "And tell you how upset our little boy was"—she pushed me a little forward—"over what happened to your son."

Mrs. Pierkowski, who had looked blank and white up until then, studied me.

"Good boy," she said, as if she had seen something. "My Alvin is playing with angels now. You will play with him maybe again someday."

This brought unbidden to my mind an image of Alvin and me making snow angels together, side by side.

After that, I don't know how long we stayed. Long enough to eat a butter tart, I suppose. Then we left the Pierkowskis' house and drove home to our trailer, Katie and I in the back seat looking in opposite directions out our windows. What she was looking for, I can't say. I took in all the main buildings of town. There were only four: the headframe of the mine, by far the tallest structure in West Spirit Lake, the marker for the rich body of gold ore that was the reason we were all there; the United Church, where I had not been made to go see Alvin lying in a snow-white casket, with its stubby steeple, not nearly as graceful as the slim arrowhead my two index fingers could form; the school, where I would never be entirely at ease, but where I would try to have only friends; and the arena, where I would become a fast skater, maybe the fastest of my age in West Spirit Lake, and where, in the last year when I might still have been thought of as just a boy, I would allow myself to hate someone again.

CHAPTER 1/

I can think of only two things sure to bring pleasure: singing out loud without concern for who is listening and running fast without much effort. Everybody knows about what singing can do. Running is another matter, but I'm one of those who can testify to its powers. During the summer when I was thirteen, I conceived of our town of West Spirit Lake mainly as a network of paths, radiating out from our house by the shoreline, all there to run on.

Nearly every day I was sent to pick up the mail from the post office. This meant loping down our short street to its dead end, bounding up the path worn into a steep embankment where cliff swallows came to pluck pieces of clay for their nests, and then hitting my stride through a sparse hillside grove of birches and scrub willows.

Within a minute I was out of the trees and into the built-up part of town nearer the plateau. Here I would slow to a jog out of deference for the other people on the sidewalk. There would not be many of them. The main street wasn't much of an attraction: the one-storey, yellow-brick post office squatted beside the grocery store, across from the two-storey building grandly called the Municipal Hall, but always referred to more plainly as the "town office." That was about it.

We never got any interesting mail. Still, the postmistress, Mrs. Kuzik, would glare at me over her glasses as if I might be collecting illicit material.

"What's your hurry?" she asked me many times, as if she meant to have an answer.

Her stare was one reason I much preferred being sent out for cigarettes.

Smoking was my mother's chief passion, apart from music. In my memory her sturdy fingers apply the same precision in tapping a piano key or a lit Craven A on the edge of a glass ashtray. I can hear our old upright and see the quarter-inch of grey ash coming off neatly. She taught piano lessons in our living room after school and on Saturday mornings. As soon as her last pupil was out the door, she would reach for her pack. If she opened it to find only foil and tobacco shreds, she would send me running. Why she never bought them by the carton, I don't know.

Unlike the mail run, a mission to purchase cigarettes offered me options. In the wintertime, I might run up to the arena and buy them at the concession counter; then I could pause to watch whatever hockey team was playing or practising.

Or I might run to the bunkhouse where the unmarried miners lived, and buy them from the snack booth in the basement recreation hall. The attraction here was the action on two big Brunswick snooker tables, always in use, and the two polished hardwood lanes for five-pin bowling. These were not modern automated lanes, so boys were needed to work as pin-setters. It paid fifty-five cents a game. That was the first way I earned money—crouching at the end of the alley with another boy, both of us leaping down to set the pins up again on our lane after a bowler had finished a frame.

You had to be nimble.

"Heads up, kid!" a miner would shout, laughing, as he sent a ball rumbling down at me before I had placed the last pin and hopped back up to my safe perch. I was never hit by a ball, but was more than once clipped by a flying pin.

That summer when I was thirteen, though, I would nearly always choose to buy Mom's cigarettes at Babcock's Marina. This was the route: down through our back yard to where the lawn ended at a swath of rocks and bush along the lakeshore, hang a left, then four hundred strides, sprinted, along a narrow mud path that skirted the water's edge.

The marina was the jewel of the Babcocks' entrepreneurial crown. Their gas station on the edge of town, the cottages they rented cheap, and a little taxi business—no doubt these were profitable. But their lakeside enterprise amounted to a near monopoly on gasoline for boats and minnows for fishing, so the cash flowed in.

Not that the marina looked like much. It consisted of a dock of rough boards with a gas pump, a few lopsided boathouses where they kept aluminum fishing skiffs for rent, a shed where Mr. Babcock shuffled around mumbling as he fixed outboard motors, and a bait-and-tackle shop with a Coke machine where Mrs. Babcock held court. She sold cigarettes there, too.

And she was enormously fat. Her taste ran to Orange Crush and Nielson's Malted Milk bars. Also Old Dutch potato chips, salt and vinegar flavour. Usually all three were arrayed on the glass counter beside her cash register, obscuring the view of filleting knives and fishing reels on display beneath.

"Craven A regulars, please," I would recite.

"I wouldn't if I were you." Here would come one of her usual lines. "Girls don't like smokers, it's like kissing an ashtray."

"They're for my mother." My reliable, deadpan answer, eyes down, though I didn't really mind this ritual.

Then sometimes Mrs. Babcock's friend, Betty Peckford, would interject. "He's not smokin 'em," she would say. "Look at him running down here at all hours, all the time. He's got wind. He's like a deer. Give him a pack."

Betty sat all day on an old couch of indeterminate colour and fishy odour beside the counter. Her voice was like a file on rusty metal. It seemed to come not so much from her throat, as from the junkyard of her mouth, all gunmetal blue fillings and caps, except for a single gold incisor—a memento of some prosperous year in her unlucky life.

They say everybody knows everything about everybody else in a small town, but that's not true. I knew only a few things about Betty. She had no husband and nobody knew exactly why he had gone or where. Her daughter Annie, some five years older than me, was pretty and wild. My mother had once called her "a little footloose and fancy free."

And I knew Betty's son had gone to prison before he turned twenty. Once, when I stepped into Babcock's to buy cigarettes, I saw Betty and Mrs. Babcock deeper in conversation than usual, neither smiling, and Betty was saying firmly, "He was always a bad boy. Always."

I guessed she must be talking about her lost son, and I have never forgotten her resignation, the repeated word. Or the sight of her. Now when I call up that image, I realize how old she looked for a mother whose two children were only just reaching adulthood.

Betty started to take a liking to me that summer when I was thirteen, and I didn't know how to feel about it. She flirted with gusto. "Sit down here for a minute," she would say, patting the space beside her on the couch vigorously, raising some bait-scented dust.

Of course I never responded, much less sat.

Or she would remark on my appearance.

"Look at those nice legs," she would rasp to Mrs. Babcock. "Why, there's not even any hair on them yet. Not enough fuzz for a bumblebee. Hey, don't run out of here so fast!"

She didn't always go on joshing that way. In fact, sometimes Betty and Mrs. Babcock would break off a hushed conversation when I came in, clearly meaning to start it up again when I was gone. More than a few times, I came to realize, music seemed to play a part in whatever they were talking about.

Once I stopped just outside the marina door, which was always ajar in the warm weather, to shake a pebble out of my shoe, and I heard Mrs. Babcock saying in a worried voice, "But that's just one of the old hymns, everybody knows it."

"But everybody doesn't sing it," Betty said. "Not outside of church. And not much outside of a funeral."

"That doesn't mean anything," Mrs. Babcock snapped back, not at all the way she usually spoke with Betty. Then they both went quiet as I slipped up to the counter. I got my mother's Craven As that day without any kidding around.

Other times the bits of conversation I caught were less urgent, and Betty's remarks didn't arouse any opposition from Mrs. Babcock. "He suddenly likes them old country songs—he's fooling around on her." (Mrs. Babcock laughs.) "Do you hear how she's always humming that nice tune that sad way? That's a woman with something to hide." (Mrs. Babcock raises her eyebrows.)

As the summer weeks passed, I found I was lingering at Babcock's Marina more than was strictly necessary. I liked to watch the fishing boats come in to be gassed up, and sometimes on breezy days I would help bring them alongside the dock without scuffing too much against the old, bald tires hanging there as cushioning. Some regular customers began to assume I was working there. They would send me up to the shop with a couple of dollars to pick up a dozen fish hooks and two Cokes while they waited for Mr. Babcock to fill their gas tanks.

If business by the dock was slow, I might putter around with Mr. Babcock in his shed for an hour as he repaired outboard motors. "God damn these damn Mercurys," he would say if he happened to be working on one. "God damn these damn Johnsons," if that was the make he had up on his bench. I would hand him a greasy screwdriver when I could see he needed one, and he would accept it as if it was entirely proper that I should be in attendance, a nurse to his surgeon.

I was never paid for any of this except in the occasional pack of gum or a dozen free minnows from the galvanized aluminum tub if I was going fishing on a Saturday with my father. Mr. Babcock would even scoop me out shiners, the rainbow-sided minnows that were more attractive to pickerel than the drab but less expensive chubs. There was never any suggestion I should pay, and Dad clearly wondered about this largesse, especially from merchants as notoriously tight as the Babcocks. "Hey, you're in pretty good with proprietors here," he would say in an admiring way. "What have you got on them?"

I would shrug. Having secrets had always appealed to me. We would cruise off in our sixteen-foot runabout, a nice boat befitting one of the town's few professionals, but not ostentatious. My father, a careful man in everything he did, maintained its eighty-horsepower outboard meticulously, so there was never occasion for me to hear Mr. Babcock cursing over our motor's spilled guts in his shed.

I came to accept Betty's watching me closely, both on my frequent appearances at Babcock's to buy cigarettes and when I was just hanging around. While I was clearly a favourite of hers, she also joked around with the other kids who came in. Especially the boys. Sometimes I was reminded of her absent husband and jailed son.

One day, it must have been well into August, I was hunting in Babcock's for some red and white daredevil lures that had been requested by a fisherman who was having his tank filled down at the dock. It was late afternoon, when the sunlight came through the marina's west-facing window, dusty and streaked as it was, and reached the wall where fishing tackle of every description hung from a big pegboard, turning it into pirate treasure. Even the greasy concrete floor shone silvery at this hour, especially in the path from the front door to Mrs. Babcock's counter, where traffic had worn it smooth. I was intent on my search and didn't look up when I heard Betty trying to get a rise out of a new customer.

"Hey, curly, where did you get those lashes?" she said. "I bet all the girls are jealous."

There was no response. Now I looked up to see who Betty was teasing. It was a boy about my age, and his hair was curly and his lashes were indeed long and dark. He was not short, exactly, but compact. I could see round biceps, the muscles of a man, bulging a little through his T-shirt, and was instantly conscious of my own slight build.

Betty kept at him. "Are you a little shy, cutie? Come and sit down and have a chat."

"You think I'm going to sit by you, you old hag? I can smell your breath from here."

Those were the first words I heard from Michel St. Vincent, who was called Mike by everybody except his mother and father. I think Mrs. Babcock told him to smarten up, or something of that sort, but she took his money and gave him what he wanted. A Coke, a package of Players. She didn't think to ask if they were for his parents.

On his way out the door—and he made a point of not hurrying—he caught me glancing at him. I thought he was going to say something, but this first time he sent nothing more my way than a black look.

He became a regular Babcock's customer, always with the same order. The cigarettes turned out to be for his father, at least some of the time. The Coke was always Mike's own. He would down it in two or three long guzzles. If I were helping out when he happened in, he would call me "minnow boy." After he heard me justifying my cigarette order one day, he never missed a chance to tell me to "hurry home to mommy."

If he was around when I was leaving the marina, I would restrain my urge to run until I was hidden by the brush along the shoreline path; for some reason I didn't want him to see me exert myself. Or if I spotted him inside at the counter before he saw me, I often loitered around outside to give him time to clear out.

One day Mike heard Betty flirting with me. From then on, whenever he saw me around town, he would say something like, "There goes Ever-Ready Betty's boy." He must have learned this nickname for her around the pool tables at the rec hall. Mike was the first boy of my age to play snooker there regularly, and he caught on fast, often playing with miners twice our age. My school friends and I had never thought ourselves old enough to even try.

Late that summer, at the end of August, and quite suddenly, I noticed that Betty stopped joking around when I came into the marina. Yet she was, if anything, even more attentive to my movements. I saw her watching me, even leaning a little forward on her ancient couch when I came in, as if she was afraid to miss something. In a way, I would have preferred her little asides about my skinny legs or my sandy hair or my grey eyes.

Then one day she spoke to me in a new voice: "What's that you're humming?" She demanded this as if I must give her an answer. No joking. I told her I wasn't humming anything. "Yes you were. But I can't catch it between your breathing, you're panting so hard." I told her again that I wasn't humming anything. Mrs. Babcock looked uneasy and handed me my mother's cigarettes before I had even asked for them.

So Betty was listening for sounds I didn't know I was making. A few days later, back in the repair shed, I asked Mr. Babcock about it.

"She's listening to you? How do you know?"

"She keeps asking what I'm singing, or humming, but I'm not singing or humming anything."

"You must be," Mr. Babcock said. "Betty listens."

Then he told me about her gift. He had first become aware of it many years before, when he was still a miner, and she told him one day that the tune he was whistling meant he was due for good luck. It was an old song from the war, and Betty explained that she had last heard it when her own father came back alive from Europe. It had been his protection as he marched through Italy. Deeply affected by the story, Mr. Babcock went out that day and placed a bet he could not afford to lose—he didn't tell me on exactly what—and it came up a winner.

"Five grand right here in my pocket, thanks to that old song," he said, patting the pockets of his coveralls as if the grubby roll of bills was tucked in there somewhere still. "That's how we bought the gas station."

He told more stories. How Betty interpreted the song one man was singing under his breath to mean that he was cheating on his wife, and he was. How she heard a baby, not yet a year old, chirping sadly in gibberish, and predicted a bad turn; a few months later the young mother had died of cancer. How Betty knew by putting together the song a teenaged boy was whistling with the one a teenaged girl was humming that they were secret lovers, a fact that was later acknowledged by all.

Even the songs on the radio gave her clues. She would take careful note of what was playing on Mrs. Babcock's transistor when a customer happened to walk in, and tell that individual's future from it.

Learning all this, I was left with no doubt that I must let Betty hear what I was humming, even though I didn't know myself, and find out what she made of it.

But how? Now that I knew the secret, wouldn't I skew the results by trying to think of a song to hum that would bring good fortune? I would have to clear my mind and let the music come through me.

I waited for my mother to run out of cigarettes. Two days later, she finally smoked her last one from an open pack. I wanted to offer immediately to run out for more, but I stopped myself— no, best to wait as always for her to ask. Finally, late that day, she did. I ran out into the evening.

It was almost September, an in-between moment. The breeze off the darkening water carried an autumn chill, but the heat of the late summer day rose up from the ground. I crossed the grass of our back yard hardly touching down. Even in the twilight I ran along the thin lakeshore path at full speed, with the branches pressing in and the undergrowth looking at that hour more blue, or even purple, than green. Flying insects touched lightly against my face as I ran through the places where they gathered, but I didn't mind. When I came out into the gravel parking lot of Babcock's Marina, I was sweaty, and as soon as I slowed my pace the coolness of the evening settled on my arms and neck.

I knew I was humming something faintly against the beat of my heavy breathing, but I willed myself not to think about it. I walked straight up in front of Betty's couch, and she looked at me without speaking, and then turned her head and tilted an ear up at me like a woman nearly deaf.

"Well?" I whispered.

In her ruined voice, Betty hummed a little refrain. "That's it," she said.

"Again," I coaxed her.

She hummed it once more, this time a little more confidently. Then I hummed along. It was a waltz, a piano piece. She thought for a while. Mrs. Babcock was waiting with an air of great respect, neither drinking from her bottle of Orange Crush, nor nibbling her Malted Milk.

"That's a song my mother plays," I offered.

"Ah," said Betty. And then after reflecting a little longer, "It means you are waiting for a partner. Someone's coming."

Mrs. Babcock asked, "To dance with him?"

"Could be, in a way," Betty said. Then she grinned at me, her ugly, friendly mouth taking over her whole face. "Don't look so worried. Getting a partner, that can't be a bad thing."

I turned stiffly to ask for the cigarettes, and then, having paid for them and accepted the change counted out by Mrs. Babcock, I took a few steps toward the door. I don't know what made me form the question I then asked before stepping outside.

"Betty, that new kid, Mike St. Vincent, what kind of songs does he sing?"

"I never heard him sing nothing."

"How about on the radio?"

"When that one comes in, it's always the news or the weather."

Then I ran home, fast, and came in a little shivery from sweating and cooling down and then sweating again. When I stepped through the door, my mother noticed me shaking slightly. She said, "You should have worn a sweater, sweetheart, it's almost fall."

"Mom, what's this song?" I hummed her the tune.

"Darling, that's Chopin," she said. "And you've got it note-perfect. Did you hear me playing that?"

"Maybe. Or Katie."

A new cigarette from the pack I had just handed her was unlit between her fingers. "You have a beautiful voice, you always did," she said. "But when you were little, you were by yourself so much that I didn't have the heart to make you sit and practise piano. You always seemed to be sitting somewhere anyway, in your sandbox or in your room."

"I like listening to you and Katie play."

"Do you? You should tell your sister, I'm sure she has no idea. Well, let me play you that one you like now."

Then she pulled some sheet music out of the piano bench and sat to play. One two three, one two three—even if I hadn't been able to hear at all I could have followed the beat by the flow of her wrists. Like wavelets coming to the shore by threes. She had switched on only the lamp above the keyboard, and as I was sitting behind her I could not make out her expression. The rest of the living room was shadowy, and the picture windows, which faced the water, reflected like mirrors so I couldn't see outside.

On a nearly still night like that close by the water, sound carries. I wondered if down the shore at the marina, Mrs. Babcock might have finally tired of the radio's din and turned it off, letting Betty catch the faint melody of the piano, knowing very well where it must be coming from.

Chapter 2/

In a really small town there will be only one of a lot of things. Only one restaurant decent enough for anniversary dinners, probably at the hotel. One bakery. A single traffic light dangling above the key intersection on the main drag, if any at all—West Spirit Lake didn't even have that.

No more than one of certain types of people, too. One guy thinks he's a riot and offers to be Santa Claus at the kids' Christmas party and master of ceremonies at wedding receptions. One woman is known for her large collection of novelty salt and pepper shakers. And one man is the town's richest—everybody knows who—although nobody thinks to figure out who is the poorest.

One old couple, after a long time together and with their children grown and gone, are the best gardeners; tomatoes ripen for them even if the growing season is really too short, as it is in West Spirit Lake.

One schoolteacher is liked best by children at the time they sit in her classroom. Of course, a sterner one is better remembered years later. One carpenter is sought out when you need some kitchen cupboards with drawers that don't stick, but the others will do for framing in a house.

As I was well aware, there might be two or three doctors, six or eight nurses, but only one pharmacist.

Only one girl who can turn into the most beautiful, and who must also then be the least knowable, no matter who she is to you. That's just the way it is, or, anyway, the way it was in West Spirit.

In our town, there was one river called the river, the one that drained into the lake closest to the town. Rivers farther away were called by their proper names. And the lake was, of course, just the lake, as surely as the sky was the sky.

And in anyone's memory, there was one sergeant to give orders to the half-dozen constables in West Spirit Lake's provincial police detachment. But this changed in that fall when I was thirteen, about the time school was starting.

Sgt. Kowalchuk, or the old sergeant, as we soon started calling him, didn't leave. But a new man, Sgt. Martin, arrived. This started some people talking. Why the sudden need for two officers at the top? Down at the marina, I heard grown-ups speculating about the possible answers. "It's the drugs," one customer said as Mr. Babcock counted him out two dozen lively shiners from his little net. "There's too much drugs in the bunkhouse. There was a time when a miner got good and drunk on payday and that was that."

Along with this theory, there was a body of opinion that had Sgt. Martin spearheading an investigation into high-grading— the practice of miners smuggling chunks of gold up from underground to sell on the black market.

High-grading was not an easy sort of stealing. Miners finishing their shifts were required to change out of their coveralls in one locker room, then walk naked through a shower to a separate change area where they dressed to go home. Only their steel lunch boxes came and went with them, and these were frequently and closely inspected. But maybe a guy bought an expensive new snowmobile, or took his wife to Florida for a nice winter vacation—and then somebody might whisper that he was seen to be walking a little funny sometimes on his way home after work.

Speculation that a second sergeant was needed to deal with some pressing crime problem in West Spirit Lake was only one school of thought, however. There was a parallel, even juicier, set of rumours. These swirled around the theory that Sgt. Martin was himself the issue, maybe a bad cop sent into exile. Again, I caught the key words around the marina.

One morning, I heard Mrs. Babcock asking Betty, "What's his poison then? What do you hear?"

"Whistling through his teeth like that, under that yellow moustache, I couldn't barely make out a damn thing," Betty grumbled. "It's girls, I guess, or money. Or both."

"Girls or money," Mrs. Babcock scoffed. "Going out on a limb here, eh?"

I asked, "Who whistles through his teeth?"

"What's this, what's this?" Betty cackled, reaching out with a bony hand as if to grab me. "The walls got ears."

I figured they had to be talking about the sergeant. Who else?

One afternoon shortly after school started in September, I dropped by my father's drugstore on my way home. Katie was already there. Her high school classes finished before my day in grade eight was done. She was, as usual, working efficiently at the cash register, looking a good deal older than sixteen. Something about the way she stood, resting her hands on the checkout counter, but never leaning on them, her shoulders pulled back slightly, but not so much that she looked stiff. She smoothly pivoted a quarter-turn as she worked, between smiling at the customer and frowning, just a touch, at the machine as she tallied up the prices. I never spent as much time around our store as Katie always did.

My father was at the back of the shop in his raised work area, from which he cocked an ear at the customers who came in to ask questions about prescriptions they needed filled. I always liked the look of him there, in his white coat, surrounded by neatly labelled jars topped with cotton and banks of white cupboards with chromed metal handles. He was a big man, and yet never looked cramped in his confined workspace.

This day when I came in, he was leaning down more intently than usual to hear what a customer was saying. Then I saw that it was no regular customer, but Mr. Brascomb, my father's predecessor as the town's druggist, the man who sold him the pharmacy.

Mr. Brascomb was retired, although he filled in for two weeks every summer when we drove south to visit my grandparents. While he seemed to enjoy these brief stints "back in harness," as he put it, I never got the sense that he resented my father's taking over his role in town. The fact that they were such different types must have made it easier. Mr. Brascomb was as slight and spry, flitting around among the pills and powders like a sparrow, as my father was stolid and deliberate.

Anyway, Mr. Brascomb had something else to keep him busy in retirement: gossip. This was a dangerous sideline for the man who had once known what medicines every person in town was taking. Years later, I was told that during Mr. Brascomb's time as town pharmacist, it was not uncommon for those in West Spirit Lake who required certain items from the drugstore to drive two hours down the highway to buy them in the next town. The arrival of my father, a man would never be taken for overly talkative, was greeted by many with a sigh of relief.

Different as they were, though, Dad liked to chat with Mr. Brascomb, or at least couldn't resist listening to him. And on this early autumn day, he was so attentive that he didn't notice me walking to the back of the pharmacy.

"... darned lucky no criminal charges were brought, I'll tell you," Mr. Brascomb was saying as I edged up. "And of course there's no further they could ship him off than to West Spirit, we're the arse end of the province. Tucked him away out of sight up here until it all blows over, I'd say."

Then my father raised his eyes and eyebrows in my direction and Mr. Brascomb broke off and pirouetted toward me. "Hey there, boy, how's school?" he chirped. I was as tall as he was, so we were looking each other in the eye. My father straightened up behind his counter on his platform, and now loomed over us both.

I was certain they had been speculating about the new sergeant. Though I had already heard snippets at the marina and some schoolyard versions of the story, this was different—just the fact that the topic was commanding my father's attention. I could see from his face that he guessed I had caught something. He was annoyed with Mr. Brascomb, no doubt, but I'm sure even more with himself for indulging in that sort of chit-chat.

"School's not what this one has on his mind," Dad answered on my behalf. "He's waiting for them to get the ice in at the arena so they can start the hockey season."

This was a typical conversational turn in our town. Any awkward moment could be defused by a mention of hockey, the universal public passion. The centre of winter life in West Spirit Lake was the arena, and it was a given that every boy was hockey mad. In my case, this was half true. Mr. Brascomb picked up the signal from my father and began to discuss how the nights were almost cold enough now for them to start thinking about cranking up the arena's artificial ice plant.

"You'll be skating by mid-October," he told me.

"That's too far off!" I complained brightly, playing my part.

So we three chatted a while about the coming season, both local teams and the National Hockey League, long enough for the uneasiness to drift away. I was thinking the whole time, though, about what Mr. Brascomb had been saying when I came in.

The very next day, as it happened, I met Sgt. Martin. From that moment on, at least for some months, Mr. Brascomb's theory that the sergeant might be a disgraced officer sent to West Spirit Lake to distance him from some unnamed scandal wasn't far from my thoughts. Here is how I first encountered him.

There was an airport carved into the bush just two miles down the highway from town. It was used by small planes flying supplies north to isolated Native reserves and fishing lodges. Also by prospectors who flew their own bush planes to the claims they were working. There was a government building with a radio room, a weather station, and a flag snapping from a pole to show that this was an official place.

We used to ride our bikes out to the airport to watch the planes take off and land. Some of my friends learned all the types—new twin-engine Beachcrafts and Otters, old single-engine Beavers and Norsemen. Once or twice rich Americans coming north to fish landed their private Lears, before transferring to small planes outfitted with pontoons for the last hop to some lakeside retreat, and we gaped at the milk-white jets they left behind resting on the tarmac.

But we had a more regular reason to visit the airport. Every Wednesday at four in the afternoon, a green van from the mine would drive out to the edge of the runway to transfer that week's production of gold to a waiting plane. In good weather, we rarely missed witnessing this operation. We knew the best place to leave our bikes in the grass and stand against the chain-link fence to watch.

The way I remember it, one man handed the gold bricks, one at a time, from the back of the van to another man, who relayed the brick to a third, who placed it carefully inside the cargo door of the small plane. Each brick was wrapped in a brown paper band with some lettering on it, but the buttery metal stuck out a few inches at each end, clearly visible from where we stood.

At least, that's my memory. I've been told that this is all wrong, that the bricks would not have been passed one by one, but by forklift on a wooden pallet. Also, a veteran of the West Spirit Lake mine dismisses my recollection that we actually saw the yellow glint; the bricks would not have been wrapped only in a strip of paper, but bundled together in a secure box.

Even my certainty that the shipment was made every Wednesday at 4 p.m. rang false to this old-timer. That would have made stealing the shipment too tempting. And, in fact, my friends and I often discussed pulling off just such a theft.

We were ruthless in our scheming. "Two guys hide in the bush at that end of the runway," one of us would say, pointing to the best place for an ambush. "When the plane slows down to turn around, we pick off the pilot and the guard from the trees. Then two more of us come down the runway"—we pictured doing this on our bicycles—"and dump the bodies and take over the plane."

Mike St. Vincent was with us at the airport on the first Wednesday in the September when we were all thirteen and had just started back at school. It was one of the few things my friends and I did that seemed to interest him. He showed a special insight into devising variations on the heist, and was sketching out one of his scenarios as we watched the gold being transferred that day.

"When the van is pulling up to the airport, one of us rides his bike in front of it and pretends to get knocked down," he explained to us. "The driver goes, 'Oh no, I hit a kid.' He says to the guard, 'Run to the airport, call an ambulance.' The guard goes. The rest of us jump the driver, tie him up, throw him in the ditch. If he makes too much fucking noise, we slit his throat."

I remember the throat-slitting part very clearly. Before then, the only violence we had envisioned in our robberies was shooting pilots cleanly from a distance.

"Then we've got the van," Mike went on. "We've got the gold, all we need to do is get the plane ..."

As he was saying all this, we were all leaning up against the fence, six or seven boys, our fingers hooked in the chain links, our eyes on the gold.

Then a baritone from behind us interrupted Mike. "But it's broad daylight. The air traffic control officer and the airport manager are waiting for the gold, watching out for the van. So of course they see the whole thing from the window of their office. By the time you have the van driver tied up, they've called me"—it was Sgt. Martin—"and I've sent three cruisers, two officers in each, heading up the highway.

"You'll never reach the plane," he carried on, "unless you're packing automatic weapons to shoot your way on. And if you can't get away by air, you'll have to make a run for it in the old van. Well, my men are driving new Ford Custom 500s with police V8s and police suspension, and we'll run you down before you've gone five miles. Best to give yourselves up."

He said these last five words with an air of deep satisfaction while affectionately patting his revolver in its polished black leather holster.

His voice, his bearing, his height. The way he kept his pale blue eyes on the van and the plane, watching the gold being transferred as carefully as we always did. Never actually looking at us all the time he was speaking. His moustache. The way he stood alert but not rigid, as if we were lined up in front of him against that fence for an inspection that would presently begin. On his time.

He paused a minute—I mean a full minute. By now we were all facing him, but I could hear the plane's engines starting behind me, and knew by the sound that the gold was now loaded and the propellers were beginning to spin.

"No, a life of crime's not going to make you rich with that kind of thinking. Now, a pro hockey contract—that's an outside possibility. Any of you boys play?" We all nodded, not speaking. "Anybody here bantam age?" That meant thirteen and fourteen years old, so we all nodded, and some of us even tentatively raised our hands. Still not one of us dared speak. "Good. I'll be your coach this year. Better come to training camp in shape."

I had never heard of hockey practice being called training camp before. It sounded serious. I wondered for a moment what had happened to the old bantam team coach if Sgt. Martin was going to be taking over. Not that I doubted he would be. And there could be only one coach, so clearly that was going to be him. Our first skate was at least a month away, but the sergeant's season had begun.

CHAPTER 3/

When you're a kid, who matters and who doesn't seems clear. There could be no doubting Sgt. Martin mattered; he was a new boulder plopped into the current. Yet it was not through his doing that I found myself mixed up with Mike St. Vincent. Icemaking was what did it, to begin with, at least, and the old man who made the ice in our town was named Julius.

Julius had not always been around. He came to West Spirit Lake the year after we moved into our new house, when I would have been only six. I remember his arrival. He took up residence on White Dog Island, which was half a mile directly across the lake from the town. His was the only cabin on the island's shore, and since our dining room window faced out over the water, we had a good lookout from which to watch him settle in.

He had showed up out of nowhere, driving a pickup truck that had once been blue. There was a load of good lumber in the back. He wasted no time buying a used aluminum skiff from Babcock's Marina, paid cash, and hauled his two-by-fours, sheets of plywood, and bundles of shingles across to the island. Smoke was seen coming from the pipe chimney of the old cabin for the first time in many years. Sounds of sawing and hammering floated over the water. Then the old man, surprisingly nimble, could be seen repairing the roof. Next, and more unexpectedly, he hung flower boxes below the two square windows that stared back at us across the lake. Geraniums bloomed.

Enough details of his life became known to satisfy curiosity. He was a widower from a pulp mill town not five hours' drive down the highway. His wife had passed away and his children moved to the city. How he learned about the vacant cabin on White Dog Island and who he purchased it from were mysteries. If anyone asked what his last name was, he said it was Latvian and even his own father could never pronounce it, so why should anybody else bother. This always won him a laugh, and nobody ever found a polite way to inquire a second time.

He had a singsong manner of talking. There were a lot of Poles and Ukrainians in West Spirit Lake, quite a few French Canadians, and a smattering of Italians, but Julius's accent was more musical than any of theirs. In a way, his talking reminded me more of the native English spoken by miners from Cape Breton, famous choir singers and kitchen fiddlers who came west to the Laurentien Shield as their island's old coal seams gave out, to try mucking out gold instead. As a child I liked to listen to them, and I came to like listening to Julius, too.

He had his own expressions. "Goody-goody," he would say with complete seriousness if something met with his approval. And he spoke of himself as if he were another person. "Now we will see what the old man wants," he might remark to Mrs. Babcock as he stepped up to her counter, before asking for a packet of Number 6 fish hooks and some sinkers. After paying, he would nod in Betty Peckford's direction, maybe even bow slightly, although whether or not he really did this is hard to say, since Julius was beginning to be stooped with age.

During his first summer, Julius fixed up his cabin. He spent September chopping wood for the coming winter. Then one Monday in early October, he arrived in town dressed in a white shirt and with his white hair slicked back like a man on his way to church who doesn't often bother going. On my run to school that morning, I happened to see him walking stiffly into the town office. He came out with the job of icemaker, with responsibility for general maintenance of the arena and the curling rink as well.

This was a serious job. Hockey and figure skating were about all that stood between West Spirit Lake's kids and outright delinquency in the wintertime, while curling was what kept much of the adult population sane through those same cold months. So somebody had to make ice in both buildings, and that ice had to be good.

Bad ice was a recent unhappy memory in West Spirit Lake. Before Julius came, many men tried their hand at making it, none with much success. Curling bonspiels ended in shouted disputes over whether the surface was too uneven to allow a proper game, and hockey players cursed the cracks that tripped them at full speed on breakaways that would surely have led to decisive goals.

Julius changed all that. His ice didn't chip or crack much under the wheeling and accelerating and snow-spraying stops of a hockey game. And a forty-pound polished granite curling stone released just so would find the mark. "Goody-goody," he would say, squinting out over a silvery, freshly flooded sheet, before a skate or a stone had marred his work. "Now the old man will have a cup of coffee."

In that fall when I was thirteen, it must have been about the middle of October, I looked out across the water to White Dog Island early one Saturday morning and saw Julius hopping into his boat. He had a dog, a white one, maybe chosen for its colour as a little joke, and the mutt's running up and down the shoreline caught my eye. The next stiff breeze would blow away the few leaves that still remained on the poplars and birches, but on this day there were still enough clinging to the branches that the island had a buttery tint. The soft warmth of the hue was a trick, though; it was cool and would soon be cold.

"You think Julius will start making ice this weekend?" I asked my father.

"Any day now," he answered. "Any day when it's not going to be too warm at midday and overtax the ice plant. The radio says it's supposed to stay below freezing all today and tomorrow. Maybe Julius will get at it this morning."

Dad always knew about such things, and was always to the point in explaining them.

After breakfast I ran up to the arena. I could see my breath, and too big a gulp of air stung my lungs a little, but I didn't mind. The parking lot was deserted except for Julius's truck. He must have arrived not long before me. The side door was open and I slipped in.

Every building in West Spirit Lake was boxy except this one; every other roof was flat or sloped not too steeply. The arena was vaulted. Ten or so massive, unpainted, wooden arches soared up over the ice surface, half circles pressed down just a little. The heavy lumber had come from trees far thicker and taller than the scraggly black spruces that grew around West Spirit Lake. It had been milled from coastal firs out in British Columbia decades ago, then trucked east at great expense by the West Spirit Lake Gold Co. Ltd. This was back when the mine was new and the men made wealthy by it were still dazed by what they had.

Julius was nowhere to be seen as I entered. The arena's empty insides made me think of the Noah's ark in a Bible storybook I had leafed through on one of the few occasions when Mom and Dad made Katie and me go to Sunday school. Except instead of warm animal smells, this place had the clean air of swept floors, exposed timber, and a fresh coat of paint on the bleachers where the crowds would soon gather to watch the games.

I walked out onto the smooth concrete where the ice would be. I stepped lightly so there would be no echoing. When I reached the centre, I looked up at the rafters. Then the melody of Julius's voice came from somewhere. "Now we see the old man has company." He shuffled out from under the stands.

"The side door was open," I said. "I just came in to find out if you were making ice."

"Goody-goody." Then he studied me for a few seconds before saying, "For the old man, please help the other boy to pull out the big hose."

The other boy. From the shadowy passageway behind Julius, Mike St. Vincent emerged, dragging a heavy black fire hose. It was stiff and dusty from being coiled up all summer.

What was he doing here? But then, did I have a better reason? The door was open. It was icemaking time. I thought of leaving, but why should I be the one to run? This was my arena, in my town, where I was known to all. Even Julius, though I had rarely spoken directly to him, would recognize me as one of the kids who had hung around watching him work in past winters. And I was the boy who sometimes scooped him out a dozen minnows at the marina on a summer day, or grabbed the prow of his boat to pull it up to Babcock's dock on a morning when the wind on the lake made it tricky to bring it in gently. Mike was the outsider.

So I remained and worked that whole morning with Julius, making ice. Mike stayed and helped out, too. We mostly listened to the muttering of the old man and didn't talk much between ourselves. Julius took his time. With the black hose he applied the first coat of water, very thin, just a glaze, over the concrete, which was cooled from beneath by an unseen grid of refrigeration tubes. When that was frozen, he covered it with another thin membrane of water, and then another. "Ice is like plywood, more layers, more strong," he told us, and then, after reflecting, "Like paint also, more coats, more smooth."

When he was satisfied with the base he had laid down, he started a small tractor, which was hitched to a two-wheeled trailer that carried two forty-five-gallon drums of water. The water flowed evenly out of the drums through a pipe punctured with many small holes. The fine spray covered the ice evenly. Julius steered the small tractor with one hand, squinting back over his shoulder at the distribution of the water.

At lunch, I went home and told my parents what I was up to.

"Julius paying you guys?" my father asked. "Or did you two decide to do this out of undiluted respect for your elders?" It bothered me that he assumed Mike and I were a team, but how could I explain that it was not really so?

When I returned to the arena in the afternoon, the building

was quiet. Now it was colder inside than outside. I looked around for Julius, and finally found him in a little room he had fixed up beneath the bleachers. He was asleep on a carpenter's bench. Near him was what was left of his lunch: a plastic container of what looked to be yogourt—an exotic food to me back then—part of an onion and the heel of a thin sausage, a sharp knife, a thermos, and a delicate-looking china cup, missing its handle, still half full of milky coffee.

On the walls were calendars with pictures of Toronto Maple Leafs and Montreal Canadiens hockey teams from past seasons. Also one from a spark-plug manufacturer showing girls in tight, short skirts and flimsy blouses, and another from a tire company on which the girls wore even less. I was looking at them when Mike slipped in.

"See anything you like?" he asked. When I spun around, he made a gesture with his fist at his crotch, which took me a second or two to understand.

Julius had woken up. "Now we see if young men like better romance or athletics," he said, yawning.

I turned to him and stammered out something about this year's Leafs lineup looking better than any of the famous old teams shown on his faded calendars. Julius shrugged with his skinny shoulders and then stretched his wiry arms. "This afternoon, the old man finishes making a little ice. Tomorrow, the boys paint on the lines."

"Us?"

"Yes. I am too old for painting lines. For lines, you have to kneel on the cold ice and keep steady and have good eyes. No. This is the difference between young and old."

Later that afternoon, after we finished the icemaking, Julius showed us cans of red and blue paint we would use the next day for the lines. He brought out some clever tools he had made for himself, with little circular blades and wheels attached to the ends of broom handles, for cutting straight grooves into the ice surface where the paint needed to go.

For some reason I had trouble falling asleep that night. Still, when Sunday morning came I woke up early and dressed before breakfast. "Take it easy," Dad said. "I can't believe Julius will be there much before eight."

But when I got to the arena, not only was the icemaker there, he already had company. Mike was in the little room under the spectator stands, stirring bright red paint with a stick. "Now we see how the old man gets lazy with plenty of helpers," Julius joked as I stood in the doorway without speaking.

I was mad at myself for letting Mike arrive before me. Yet I didn't know why it mattered. Julius soon put me to work mixing blue paint as Mike continued with the red. Then he directed us out onto the ice where he had incised lines precisely where he wanted the colours laid down. First he kneeled and showed us what he wanted. Even. No drips. No ripples. Follow the straight grooves he had cut.

He trusted us, though, once we got started. I believe he even allowed himself to doze a little as he sat in the stands overseeing our progress, sipping now and then from his handleless coffee cup. Mike painted the wide red line at centre and then the thinner red lines marking the goal creases and the face-off circles. I worked a little more slowly, painting the blue lines that in hockey mark the borders between the neutral zone and the ends of the rink where most of the action takes place.

Afterwards, we went up into the stands and looked down at what we had done. I sat on one side of Julius, and Mike on the other. The blue of the blue lines looked dense, and deep enough to plunge your arm into up to the elbow at least. The red was red enough to imagine heat coming off it. "Goody-goody," said the old man. Sitting so long in the chill seemed to have left him sleepy.

"It's like it's almost too bad that we're going to skate on it," I ventured.

"Don't be a suckhole," Mike said. "I can't wait to get out on it."

"Me too," I said, and then was immediately sorry I'd reversed myself.

"Hockey ice is not so hard to make," Julius mused. "Curling ice is more difficult. For curling ice, you need small bumps, delicate like on good leather." He hunted for the word and found it: "Pebbled."

Mike said, "Curling is so fucking boring."

Julius ignored this, or didn't hear. He was talking about the ice itself, not the game played on it.

"For curling ice, small bumps," he repeated. "Like a thousand thousand thousand little pearls. Spilled out."

The old man put his hands out above his knees, splayed his skinny fingers, and moved them side to side like he was spreading this imagined treasure evenly on a plane in front of him.

"Then if you wet the pearls with water, just so the little bumps get frozen, that would be good curling ice."

Even Mike didn't know what to say to this. We leaned forward at the same moment and glanced at each other across Julius, then away again, embarrassed to be hearing his private reverie.

It was then, scanning around the wooden cavern of the arena, that I noticed that we three were not quite alone. Over one end of the ice was a horizontal row of windows where you could watch a bit of a hockey game from the warmth of the arena lobby. The lobby lights were not on, but I could see someone standing at one of the windows. It was a big man and for a second I thought it might be my father.

But just as I raised my hand, I realized, no, it couldn't be. The way a man stands is as much him as his face is, and my father did not stand like that. He wouldn't have lingered there at the glass so long without coming out to say hello and ask how the work was going, either. The man who was watching turned and marched away from the window. I can't say if he had noticed my half-wave or not. He may have seen my eyes turned toward him, but I couldn't make out his.

"The new sergeant," said Mike.

"Ah," said Julius. "The authorities."

That seemed to change the air around us, and Julius rose to go, gingerly, the way old people do when they are thinking about their backs and knees. Mike and I walked out to his truck with him.

"Julius," I asked, "why don't you bring your dog over here with you? Nobody would care if you had a dog to keep you company in the arena."

"She lives on her island," Julius said. "This island even is named for her."

"Bullshit," said Mike. "It's been White Dog Island forever."

"How would you know?" I said. "You just moved here."

But he was right, of course, as far as it went. It had been White Dog Island forever, or might as well have been. The next day I went to ask the school librarian about it. Mrs. Lund was also our amateur local historian, and sometimes she came into classrooms with stuff she collected—hand-webbed Indian snowshoes, old maps, and kerosene lanterns—to try to interest kids in the pioneer days. It occupied her time, I supposed, since it was known that her husband had died in a mine accident not long after she came to West Spirit Lake to marry him. Since then she had been alone. Yet she stayed on.

I found her standing behind the library checkout desk, sorting magazines. My question made her rock on the balls of her feet, causing her smells to waft over to my side of the desk. There was hairspray—not perfume, I knew the difference from paying attention when my mother dressed to go out—and the hard mint that she was forever clicking against her teeth.

"There are two theories," Mrs. Lund began. "One is that the island was named for a ritual performed by the local Ojibwa every spring, when they would boil a pure white dog and devour it." She waited for a reaction and I gave her my best wide eyes. "The second theory," she continued more matter-of-factly, "is that the first white inhabitant of the island, a prospector in the time of the early mineral exploration, owned a white dog."

I was strongly inclined to believe the first story. But the second, though more mundane on the surface, made an impression too: that first lonely prospector's white dog must somehow be the direct ancestor of Julius's. Or so I imagined it.

From our dining room window, I had often watched the old icemaker and his dog parting company in the morning over on their island. And not just me. My mother liked to look out across the water, too, after she had lit her first cigarette of the day, the coffee perking on the stove. Katie and I would be eating toast. Dad would already be gone to open the drugstore for the day. I would follow my mother's gaze and wonder what she was thinking about. If it was a warm day and the windows were open, we might even hear the dog; there would be a slight pause between the moment when it lifted its head to yelp and when the sound reached us. Then, as Julius pulled away from his dock, came the two-stroke drone of his outboard, growing louder as he approached our side of the channel.

Mike wouldn't have cared about anything like the way an animal can be the emblem of a place, or the way a particular island can keep attracting white dogs. He might have been interested, I thought, in the information that such dogs were once boiled and eaten in this country. But I was not going to be the one to let him in on it.

CHAPTER 4/

When I remember the people who once meant so much to me, and some who still do, it is not the face or eyes that I see first or most clearly. My mother's fingers I can picture easily and exactly. My sister's hair, even though it changed over the years. My father is an exception to this rule: I see him whole or not at all.

When I call up Sgt. Martin, his mouth appears before anything else.

After that Sunday when he watched Mike and me helping Julius prepare the ice, six days passed before I saw the new sergeant again. Once again, it was at the arena, but this time in one of the basement dressing rooms. He was wrapping black tape around a hockey stick. He peeled off a long strip from a new black roll with a sound like canvas being ripped. Then he coiled it around the end of the shaft, stretching it very tight, before baring his teeth and biting off what he needed.

As I walked in he paused and smiled at me with those same teeth. "Where's your friend?"

I only looked at him so he elaborated.

"Where's your buddy, the other rink rat who was helping out with the ice last weekend?"

I came close to saying, he's not my buddy, but caught myself in time. "I don't know," I said. "Maybe he forgot when first practice was."

"Nobody forgets the start of training camp," Sgt. Martin corrected me, the ends of his moustache dipping down in a way that exaggerated his frown. "You've got permission to go find him."

I didn't want to go searching for Mike St. Vincent on a cold Saturday morning. I stood in the doorway of the dressing room, looking around at my friends. A dozen kids of every size half undressed, strapping on old padding over their long johns, and lacing up skates handed down from their big brothers, even in a few cases from their fathers. Hockey equipment back then was still leather, not yet bright plastic and nylon, and the gear was often named after animals. Black Panther was a popular model of skate. On the thumb of our gloves, to signify a hard shell, was a little picture of an armadillo. Eagles with spread wings were emblazoned on my shin guards over my kneecaps.

Boys need totems. I was always nervous before a game or even a practice, and the ritual of putting on my equipment, with all the buckling and lacing and pinching snaps, calmed me down. The birds and animals helped somehow. When the sergeant ordered me to go find Mike, I longed to just plunk down at my place on the bench, dump my equipment out on the floor in front of me, and start dressing. Instead, I had to abandon my duffle bag there and turn back outside alone.

In West Spirit Lake, everybody knew where everybody else lived. There were just five residential streets with back alleys laid out neatly on the plateau between the gold mine and the public school. This was where the underground miners and their wives and children were assigned housing. Down by the lake, a few more streets, including the one we lived on, followed the contours of the shoreline. This was where the mine management and the town's small allotment of professionals and its smattering of service workers were clustered together.

The St. Vincents lived up in the main grid in a house identical to the ones rented out by the company to all its miners. I had never been to Mike's house, but I knew exactly how it would look because I had visited lots of others just the same. The front door that opened into the small living room would almost never be used; everyone would come and go through the back kitchen. There would be no dining room. The three bedrooms would be all about the same size, but the one that had a window on the front was for the parents, with children sleeping in rooms that faced the back alley. Mike would have one of his own because, like me, he had only one sister and no brothers.

As I came up the back alley behind the St. Vincents' little house, something looked wrong. The kitchen door was not properly closed. I could see that it was open a few inches, and on a late fall morning like this one, almost early winter, the heat would rush out and the cold slip in. That was the door I had been planning to knock on, but going up to it when it was strangely ajar made me feel uneasy. So I paused by the St. Vincents' back gate and wondered what I should do.

Another thing. Saturday morning was in all my experience a busy time. Yet as I watched the back of the house, I couldn't see anyone moving around in the kitchen. And from that oddly open door, I couldn't hear any clatter of cutlery or the sound of a radio playing by the kitchen sink. Why wasn't Mike's mother bustling around making breakfast or at least coffee? If he had slept in, wouldn't she by then be fixing him a quick plate of toast or a bowl of cereal at least? Instead, there was dead quiet, apart from the intermittent tick-ticking of the clothesline against its rusty pulleys in the light, cold breeze. A couple of stiff dishrags were hanging from it. Was it possible the whole family was still sleeping and the door had been left open all night?

Just then Mr. St. Vincent came around the corner of his house, stepping lightly, as if he were stalking an animal. He had on a shirt and pants. No coat. His feet were in slippers and I could see his ankles. No socks. Dangling from his left hand was a brown belt, an old-fashioned thin one, like my grandfather wore, long enough that its tapered end just touched the blades of frost-bitten grass. The other end was wrapped tight around his fist, so he must have been clutching the buckle in the palm of his hand.

I had seen Mike's father before around town. He was short but squarely built. Back then we had two stock descriptions for a man of his stature: a fire hydrant or a brick shithouse. Seeing him moving with such stealth, though, neither of these images fit. Mr. St. Vincent had a beer gut but he was unmistakably athletic. I later learned that he was one of the fastest-working men on the end of a heavy drill in the West Spirit Lake Gold Mine, and that other miners were eager to be partnered with him since he always made his bonus, no matter how adverse the conditions underground.

I dropped to a crouch, hoping he would not see me behind the rickety picket fence that separated the little back yard from the alley. I tucked my chin down and exhaled into the collar of my coat so the fog of my breath wouldn't give me away. Luckily, his attention was elsewhere. He crept along the back wall of his house. When he reached the corner, he jumped around with the belt readied like a sling. But nobody was hiding on the other side. He swore in French and then turned, now walking normally, not poised or predatory, back to the open kitchen door. He paused before going in, hitched up his pants, which were sagging down without the belt, and looked like he might shout something. But then he stepped inside without opening his mouth. The slamming of the door was shockingly loud, setting off the neighbour's dog, whose barking was taken up by another further down the alley.

I stayed down on my haunches. If I stood up now, I might be spotted from the kitchen window. Then I heard a rattling very near me, and was about to bolt when I realized that beneath the rattle was a stifled laugh. Two garbage cans were standing by the fence and the top of one now wobbled slightly. Mike's brown eyes, Iroquois or Asian, looked out at me. His nose was just at the edge of the can and he looked ridiculously like a Kilroy Was Here drawing.

"He gone?"

"He's inside. I can't tell if he's watching."

"If he's inside, the old bastard's given up."

Mike jumped out now like a stage magician who has freed himself from chains. The din he caused with the lid made me wince. I almost expected him to take a bow, but instead he stretched like a cat. I was still cowering by the fence, so now he was looking down at me.

"Don't worry, once he gives up, he gives up."

So I straightened up, feeling foolish.

Mike opened the lid of the second trash can and pulled out his hockey bag. His stick was lying on the ground nearby, and he picked it up and put it over his shoulder. His old brown skates, tied together by their laces, dangled from its blade end like a pair of partridges. He began to walk down the alley and I hurried to fall in step beside him.

"The new sergeant sent me out to look for you. You're late for practice."

"Tell him I was sleeping," Mike said. "My mother forgot to wake me up, or something—goddamn her. You had to pull me out of bed yourself. I didn't have time even for a mouthful of coffee."

He smiled widely at this, either amused by the image of me pulling him out from under his covers, or simply by the act of making up a good lie. I wondered if he really drank coffee. He seemed completely at ease, as if spending who knows how long— a few minutes? a cold hour?—on a Saturday morning holding his breath in the dark, stale stink of a metal garbage can to elude a whack with a belt was all in a day's work.

"What was up with your dad?"

"I stole twenty bucks from his pants last night. I figured he'd had enough to drink that this morning he wouldn't remember how much he'd had in his pocket. But the son of a bitch must have stayed pretty sober for once, Christ knows why."

"What'd you take the money for?"

"Gambling debts. The eight ball hasn't been falling for me lately."

I couldn't think of anything more to say as I contemplated this magnificent reason for needing quick cash. I pictured Mike showing up that evening at the rec hall, peeling off bills from his stolen twenty by the light hanging low over the pool table to pay off what he owed, fair and square. Then, with his credit good again, he would begin casually chalking up his cue stick, while one of the men racked up the red balls for a new game, saying to Mike, "Your break."

We walked along side by side until we reached the arena. I let him set the pace and he wasn't hurrying. But once we were in the dressing room, now empty, he was all business. He pulled on his equipment efficiently, not talking. I had to rush faster than I liked to strap on my gear in time to reach the ice alongside him. I didn't want Mike joining the other guys, and Sgt. Martin, before me.

The hallway from the arena's basement dressing rooms to the ice was carpeted with a worn, black rubber, conveyor belt. It had been salvaged from the mine, where it previously carried crushed ore, and laid over the concrete floor to save skate blades from being dulled. Dim bulbs lit this passage and there wasn't much ventilation; the smells of ancient sweat and mildewy leather lingered there. At the end of the corridor was a narrow stair that climbed from the basement's murkiness up to the arena's air and light.

Then came that first stride on skates of the season. And another ten, twenty, fifty, around the rink, close to the boards. The deeper rasping as you accelerate, the fainter hissing when you glide. The scissors sound when you sharply change directions, crossing one skate over the other, leaning, resisting the tug that wants to yank you out of your arc, trusting your own strength and balance to keep pulling you further and further into the turn.

Mike and I were left to circle the ice two or three times to warm up before Sgt. Martin acknowledged us with a toot on his whistle. "You two girls finished dancing?" he said. "We've got a practice going on over here." He had the team lined up against the boards at one end of the rink, and they already looked whipped. What had happened before we joined them? They were all panting, some doubled over, trying to catch their breath.

The boy who had always been the fattest in our class at school looked as if he might throw up, he was so white in the face.

"We've been having a little skate here," Sgt. Martin said. "To see who spent the summer eating chips and watching TV. Since you two have decided to join us late, you can lead the next drill. It's puck to the corner, two guys in, and the one who doesn't come back to me with the pill gives me his best two laps."

So he slapped a puck down the length of the ice into the far corner and, after hesitating for a half-second, Mike and I chased it. I was faster. In fact, I was the swiftest skater of my age in town, and the arrival of Mike, I was glad to discover, had not changed that. But when I reached the puck first and pivoted to lug it back up the ice, Mike was right behind me. He raised his arms slightly and smashed me back into the boards. I crumpled and by the time I had struggled to my knees, and then found my feet again, he was halfway back down the ice with the puck on his stick, ragging it casually to show he had no fear of my catching up with him.

"Two of your best," Sgt. Martin shouted at me, and so I began skating around the rink, my legs wobbly. As I did my laps, my head slowly cleared. The drill was performed over and over again with Sgt. Martin sending down pairs of well-matched players. They had all seen how Mike handled me, so the strategy for the chase-and-retrieve game was set. The first guy to reach the puck turned and braced himself as the second tried to flatten him. But nobody could hit as hard as Mike.

The practice was the most gruelling any of us had experienced. The sergeant demanded that we skate all out for every drill. And he gave the stronger players plenty of chances to throw their weight at the weaker. At that age, a few of the boys I grew up with were already inheriting the bodies of their miner fathers, while others among us would not have looked out of place swinging on a swing or playing with toy trucks in the sand.

Near the end of the two hours of ice time, my legs felt as though they might not continue to hold me up, and I was looking to the clock for freedom. Sgt. Martin lined us up against the boards one more time. "Good work, men," he said, the first time he had praised us as a group. "Good start. We've got one more drill. I call this one the fox and the hound." Then he pointed his stick at me and said, "Fox." And at Mike and said, "Hound." Then he explained. The fox starts skating around the rink, and the hound is released after his quarry has a half-lap head start. The hound's job is to catch the fox. The fox's is to try to outlast the hound.

"Now, just to make things interesting," he smiled, "the rest of you girls are going to hold your sticks out like this until our hound runs down our fox." At this point, Sgt. Martin extended his own stick out parallel to the ice in one hand. Nobody could do this for long before his shoulder muscles would start screaming. All our teammates did as the new sergeant did. And then he put his whistle between his teeth with his free hand and blew a note, nodding at me, and off I went. When I had skated about a quarter of a lap, I heard another toot on the whistle and I knew Mike was after me.

I skated in a state of confusion. Sgt. Martin had to have seen that I was faster than Mike. How could he expect the slower skater to catch the faster? Did he want me to slow down on purpose, to let the game end and give my friends relief from the pain that was now building in their outstretched arms? Was the test really about sacrificing my own pride for the team? But when I did ease up a little, letting Mike gain on me, Sgt. Martin barked, "The hound's on your tail, fox, that the best you can do?"

So I bore down again. Soon the burn in my muscles was matched by a sort of mental heat, a fever I directed toward the sergeant. He didn't feel it. He stood easy, holding his stick out as if it were weightless. But I could hear my teammates. "Go, Mike, go," they groaned. "Get him, get him, get him." When I passed the row of players, arms and sticks extended in a sort of miserable salute, I could see some of them were now unable to match the sergeant's rigid posture. They were letting their sticks droop slightly, or using their free arm to prop up the one that was by now shot through with pain. "Hey, hey, I see some cheating there, girls," Sgt. Martin said. "Cheaters are going to be warming the bench on this team."

It took many laps for Mike to catch me. I was faster, but in the end he had more determination. No doubt that's how the sergeant had sized us up when he pitted us against one another. I did not intentionally slow down to finish it. Mike's incentive to catch me was far greater than mine to keep ahead of him. By the time it was over, only about half the team were still holding their sticks out. But Sgt. Martin never looked bothered himself by the test he had set. And the way he ignored the boys who had failed it—did it mean that he sympathized with them or disdained them? "Good run, fox," he said to me, and I felt—though I resisted it—a rush of satisfaction. "Good run, hound."

That was the end of our first practice with the new sergeant. We skated slowly to the gate in the boards, Mike and I spent, the rest of the guys shaking and flexing the pain out of their arms. I noticed for the first time that Julius was sitting alone in the stands, watching, something he rarely did. He made the ice but didn't often bother to stick around for the action, retreating to his little room to putter with his equipment and sometimes read. I looked up at him now as I left the ice, and I think he might have been shaking his head just a little. But Julius's gestures were so vague that I could never be certain of them. I'm pretty sure, though, that he raised his china cup to me a half-inch off his knee in a kind of tribute.

In the dressing room, everybody cheered up quickly. "Check it out," said our fat kid. "I'm already starting to bruise." The pale blue shadow on his shoulder would surely spread and darken to an uglier purple. The rest of us started looking for marks of our own to show what we had been through. Only Mike didn't boast of hits he had taken and given. He sat quietly, removing his equipment and placing each piece of gear with care in his duffle bag, revealing by stages a muscled torso and limbs that looked capable of absorbing any number of blows. And of dishing many out. I felt my whole frame starting to ache at once, mostly, I thought, from that first hard hit he gave me after we joined the practice late.

The torture of the final fox-and-hound drill was now being

joked about. "You could have slowed up a little," our skinniest kid said to me. "My arm feels like day-old dog shit." Everybody guffawed at this. But nobody was holding it against me that as the fox I had skated my fastest for as long as I could. They knew I had to keep going, and would have done the same in my place. We were all playing by the same rules now.

Chapter 5/

I was sure Sgt. Martin would eventually run into my mother at school. Other than kids and teachers, the two of them spent more time there than anyone else. There was no real reason for me to worry about them meeting up, but I did anyway while I was waiting for it to happen.

As the town's one piano teacher, my mother was in school almost every day in the last weeks of the year, helping out with the preparations for the big Christmas concert. She let the teachers run the show, but was always hovering in the wings, accompanying classroom choirs on an old upright piano, mouthing the familiar words with her lipsticked mouth. I was secretly proud of the way she had with kids. Seven-year-olds sounded ten talking to her, thirteen-year-olds almost grown up.

The new sergeant had quickly become a fixture in the school as well, showing up often in classrooms to tell little kids about traffic safety or older ones about the dangers of drugs. Sgt. Kowalchuk had never been much good at this sort of thing; Sgt. Martin was a natural. Taller and broader than any teacher, he stood still at the very centre of the front of a class, his pale eyes sweeping the room. Everybody listened carefully and tried to think up serious-sounding questions to ask. He also launched an anti-vandalism campaign, enlisting our principal, Mr. Kenison, who loved causes of any sort.

The inevitable encounter happened in late November, about six weeks after our hockey practices began.

I knew my mother would be in school on that particular day for a meeting of the Christmas concert committee. The theme for the production that year was "A Huron Carol," the hymn written to an old French tune by Father Brébeuf before he was martyred by the Iroquois. It happened to be my favourite Christmas song, and Mom told me the show would feature the nativity story acted out by little kids in headdresses, furs, and face paint. For a manger, there would be a wigwam made of old bedspreads. She had been playing the song on the piano in our living room the night before, scribbling ideas for the show on foolscap, as I sat on the couch listening.

'Twas in the moon of wintertime,
When all the birds had fled,
That mighty Gitchi Manitou
Sent angel choirs instead

Those opening lines never failed to draw me in. Next comes the part about "a lodge of broken bark," instead of a manger; the swaddling clothes become "a ragged robe of rabbit skins." But what I liked best was that in place of the shepherds watching their flocks by night were "wandering hunters." My mother sang rather formally, in a manner left over from childhood voice lessons, her tone tarnished only slightly by the years of cigarettes:

But as the hunter braves drew nigh
The angel choir grew loud and high
Jesus your King is born, Jesus is born,
In excelsis gloria.

For the braves to emerge like that from the forest to pay their respects to a fat baby nestled in white rabbit skin was something to think about. How many times had I played in the scrub willows along the lakeshore, slipping through shadows with a knife (imaginary) dangling at my hip in a fringed sheath, and a rifle (a stick) held low in one hand?

I had the song on my mind as I stood alone in the school hallway late the following afternoon, waiting for my mother's concert meeting to end. Afterwards, we were going over to the drugstore together to see if Dad and Katie were ready to head home. But just as she came out of the teachers' lounge, Sgt. Martin stepped out of the principal's office directly across the hall. For a second they looked at each other, and it seemed to me that something was going to happen, I'm not sure what, but this feeling dissolved almost before I was sure I felt it.

"Coach Martin," my mother said, ignoring his police rank and assigning him a title I hadn't heard anybody else use. "My son talks of nothing but your team. You'll have to let me in on your secret so I can get that kind of devotion out of my piano pupils."

"Very nice to meet you," Sgt. Martin said. "I'll tell you, if half of my guys skated half as fast as your young man, I wouldn't have to work them half as hard."

As he said this, he reached out as if to ruffle my hair—not the sort of thing he usually did—but I shifted just enough that his hand wouldn't reach, and he let it drop on my shoulder. He allowed it to rest there as if that was what he had meant to do all along. His hand had a kind of dead weight to it, with no grip from the fingers. Then he lifted it away. My mother reached out with both her hands, put one on either shoulder, and gave me a squeeze. I was hers.

"Oh, this one's a little too fast for my liking," she joked. "And growing up too fast, too, so don't you be one of those who rushes him, Coach Martin, nor my daughter, either." She wagged a finger at him theatrically.

"No, ma'am."

That *ma'am* was a little much. His voice sounded thick when he said it, as though he had trouble getting the word out of his throat. I was watching his mouth when he said it, and for the first time I saw that his lip, under his moustache, was plump, like a pouty kid's.

But that was all there was to the encounter. Nothing really. Yet as my mother turned me to walk out to the car, I knew that she had ended the encounter a little abruptly. She always made all she could of the chance to chat with any grown-up who took an interest in Katie or me. Gather intelligence. Pass along advice in her casual way. Boast a little. None of this had passed between her and the sergeant. She didn't like him, and I sensed that he felt the chill, too.

Later that evening she asked me about him. I was in my pajamas, passing by the living room where she was seated again at the piano, going over books of Christmas songs, and she called me in. "I Saw Three Ships Come Sailing In" was open in front of her. The sailing ships, so unlike the images that decorated the rest of the Christmas sheet music, stood out on the page. She played that one often, and I associated it with the way she loved getting out in our little fishing boat in the summer, and with the long minutes she spent gazing out over the water.

"Your new coach, do you think he's a little rough on you kids?" she asked me. "I heard that one of you boys threw up in the dressing-room toilet after practice. Is that true?"

"Who told you that?"

"It doesn't matter. I'm just asking if you think Coach Martin might be working you too hard, or letting things get a little too rough. Dad could talk to him."

"No way."

"No. I guess not. Well, you use your judgement. I don't want you getting hurt, and neither does your father."

"What does Dad say about it?"

"Easy does it now, sweetheart. He doesn't say anything. He just heard around the store that your new coach might be letting things get a little rough." Then she changed the subject, but not entirely: "Anyway, if you like him, I'm sure he's fine. He made an impression on your sister and her friends, too, with his last talk at the high school on vandalism. Quite an impression, I'd say. A preacher at heart."

Katie hadn't mentioned it to me. But then she didn't tell me much, or Mom and Dad, either, as far I as could figure. I wondered how Mom had gleaned that Sgt. Martin had impressed her. My mother had a way of getting at things.

In fact, she was right to be anxious about our hockey practices. They had stayed as tough as the new sergeant's first one. The team had quickly divided into two camps. The larger faction was with the sergeant all the way, but a few others were not saying much in the dressing room anymore. I was in-between. Our fat kid looked near tears as he silently strapped on his equipment, bracing himself for another session of struggling to keep up. *Sweat it off,* was the sergeant's stock advice to him. Our two smallest guys, brothers not quite a year apart in age, who were often mistaken for twins, clung even closer together than before, sharing their fear of being hurt in the hard going. The sergeant urged them to show some grit, rhyming off the names of professional players who were small but could still, as he said, *mix it up.*

Once the season started for real, there could be no more doubt about the sergeant's grip on our team. In our first few games, we beat a succession of teams from the bigger towns down the highway. We hit harder than in past years, but also skated faster. We had fewer players on our bench than most of our opponents, but we were in better shape. I could feel it in my own stride. Mike St. Vincent scored more than half our goals. He was our best player and our fiercest, and even I couldn't deny it.

After a few wins, the town started talking. Even Katie and her friends began showing up to watch. As always, Mr. Brascomb was an expert on whatever everybody found interesting. He talked about us with the air of an insider. "You guys have real momentum," he told me one day at the back of the drugstore. "Your dad here's getting a swelled head."

This was not true, I knew, since my father showed no concern at all about whether we won or lost. Not that he missed a single game. He would take his place, high up in the stands near the rafters, whenever we played. But he only put down his Styrofoam cup of coffee to clap for a really key goal—sometimes even one scored by the other team. Unlike most of the other dads and plenty of the moms, I could never pick out his voice from the many urging us on.

One day around this time, at the back of the drugstore, Mr. Brascomb pressed me a little for useful inside info. "What's doing the trick for your team this year?" he asked. "That new kid Mike, or is it the sergeant's coaching?"

"A little of both, I guess."

"The two key ingredients, talent and leadership," Mr. Brascomb philosophized. "And chemistry, eh? That's half the battle in sports, take it from an old chemist." Then, not to leave me out of his analysis, he added, "You and Mike are good chemistry, too, I'd say. A fast guy and a tough guy. A guy with finesse and a guy with guts."

Mike and me again. I slipped away from Mr. Brascomb while he was still talking about us. Mike and me. It was just his way of seeing things. Contrasts figured in all his stories. "She's a sweet, trusting soul," he might say about a woman whose marriage was the current subject of speculation. "But he's a real hard egg." Hard eggs were always paired up in his gossip with trusting souls.

I knew well the way he told his tales. Mr. Brascomb not only dropped by the drugstore often, but also appeared about once a month at our kitchen table. He was our one regular dinner guest. This started soon after we moved to West Spirit Lake, when my father was still learning the ropes of running the drugstore. He spent a Saturday afternoon sitting with Mr. Brascomb at our dining room table, going through pharmaceutical brochures and supply catalogues for toothpaste, wart remedies, and nail polish.

"You men will have to move those papers if I'm going to serve you supper," my mother said.

"Not on my account," protested Mr. Brascomb. Then he quickly added, to make sure nobody imagined he was declining the offer of a meal, "I'm happy to sit in the kitchen with the family."

So that's the way it began, and that's the way it continued. When he came, we ate in the kitchen, as if it were any old supper. He also insisted that he preferred ordinary food, and my mother obliged by bringing out homey fare, casseroles and stews, instead of the roasts and steaks that were more properly company meals. I suppose this fit with Mr. Brascomb's compare-and-contrast way of looking at the world: you were either no trouble or you were a bother.

He was, however, a bit of both. We put on a little show of not putting on a show for him. Mom would bring the hot dish to the table and spoon it out onto the everyday plates, but she would garnish the baked turkey and noodles with parsley, something she never troubled with for just us. Dad wouldn't go so far as to mumble grace, as he might have for Thanksgiving dinner or if Grandma and Grandpa were visiting, but he would make a point of waiting until everyone was served before digging in, a courtesy we didn't normally observe among only us four.

We indulged Mr. Brascomb in his view of himself as "part of the furniture," though not without limits. Katie and I couldn't bring ourselves to call him, as he once or twice suggested, "Uncle Rick." He was a mister, not an uncle. Even the Rick part never really took in our house. Mom called him Richard. This was typical, though. She had her own way of talking, and her habit was to call Daves *David* and Dons *Donald*. I noticed that men seemed to take this as a private joke, a sort of compliment. She was pretty, and her hair stayed blonde without dye well into middle age.

I cannot be sure when I started listening carefully to Mr. Brascomb's stories. It could have been from the start, when I was little. They were always the kind of observations meant to interest adults, but he was careful to tell them in such a way that Katie and I didn't have to be sent out of the room.

"Isn't it too bad that Carrie Kenison is having to go to Florida on her own this year," went one of his tidbits, memorable to me because it involved our principal and his wife. "I guess Ben couldn't take the time away from work. Still, it's nice she's able to get away by herself." My parents locked eyes for a quarter-second, conveying: now, that's odd. They hadn't heard. Katie and I glanced at each other, too, very fleetingly, and equally poker-faced, trying not to appear so interested that the adults at the table might suspect we caught the gist of the anecdote.

Just a few nights after Sgt. Martin and my mother met at school, it was time for Mr. Brascomb's monthly meal. He seemed distracted. His stories didn't go anywhere as he poked at his meatloaf. His scalloped potatoes congealed untouched. I thought I caught him looking at me in particular out of the corner of his eye over the table. Then at Katie. When desert came, Jell-O studded with mandarin orange pieces, he tried to perk up a little.

"Now this hockey season, it's looking like one for the record books," he started, and then turned squarely toward me. "You boys have one heck of a squad there, and a heck of a coach, I'd say."

"For sure," I answered. "We're going all the way."

"Attaboy, I bet you are." Now he directed himself to Mom and Dad. "Have you gotten to know the new sergeant much? He seems like such an influence on the kids."

"I met him for the first time just this week," Mom said. "At the school. He was in about the vandalism problem ..."

"That's wonderful, wonderful," Mr. Brascomb said, veering away from a potentially juicy chat about spray-painted swear words and broken beer bottles in the playground. That wasn't like him. He had something else on his mind. "But isn't it interesting about the new sergeant's living arrangements?"

My parents' blank looks showed that they didn't know anything about Sgt. Martin's living arrangements. Mr. Brascomb continued with rising gusto.

"About him moving out to the Blue Heron," he said. "I mean, why the motel when the police all get those nice apartments subsidized by the province? Seems like a lot of money to spend out of your own pocket when you don't have to."

Katie and I were looking down at our food, trying to be invisible, hoping to hear the next bit of intelligence. I chewed unnecessarily. Katie tried to divide her Jell-O into cubes with the edge of a spoon. Dad was now looking meaningfully at Mr. Brascomb, who wasn't catching on.

"The sergeant is a single guy, after all," Dad said. "Do you know a bachelor who wouldn't go to some extremes to avoid doing his own dishes and vacuuming? Room service must sound pretty sweet."

That Mr. Brascomb was himself a bachelor didn't enter into this. He made a little fluttery gesture with all his fingers, as if he was clearing my father's distracting theory from the air over the table.

"I'm sure, I'm sure. Somebody to make his bed, breakfast in the coffee shop, very nice," he said. Then he got to his point. "And there's privacy, of course. In an apartment right here in town, everybody knows who comes and goes. But with a room out there on the highway at the Blue Heron, well, there's not so many eyes around."

Now my father was glaring, and my mother spoke.

"Speaking of making beds," she said, turning to Katie and me. "Shouldn't you two go tidy your rooms, unless you've still got homework to attend to?"

This was very weak. We hadn't been sent off to clean our rooms since we were little kids, and she knew we took care of our homework right after school.

But Katie surprised me by jumping up immediately, as if she were happy to get away from talk of the sergeant, relieved to be given an excuse to escape to her own room. So I had no choice but to go to mine. I lay down on my bed and wondered why the new sergeant had moved out to the motel, and why everybody seemed to want to talk about him. Even Mom was curious about our hockey practices.

After a while I must have dozed off in my clothes. A touch on my shoulder brought me up from a dream where I was having trouble breathing and hearing, and I was chilled.

Mom said, "Get into your PJs, darling, and brush your teeth."

"What time is it?" I asked.

"Almost midnight."

"Did Mr. Brascomb go home?"

"An hour ago. Dad and I stayed up talking."

"What about?"

"Nothing. The 'Huron Carol' show."

I doubted this was true. But I went along with her, asking, "You have any new ideas for it?"

"None since last night," she smiled. "Think you'll like it?"

"How are you going to make snow on stage?"

"I don't know. Confetti and cotton balls, I suppose."

"It's weird," I said. "There'll be lots of real snow outside by then, but you'll have to fake it inside."

"It is weird," she agreed. "Now put on your pajamas and brush your teeth."

Then she kissed me on the forehead and was gone. I didn't get up right away. I lay there wondering if Sgt. Martin, alone in his motel room, had fallen asleep in his uniform, maybe with the TV on. I wondered about Katie on the other side of the wall. I imagined that Mike, after a late evening of shooting pool, was slipping back into his house, quietly, to avoid waking his father. And then I thought about the hunter braves moving through a snowy forest, by starlight, toward something they couldn't be sure about but wanted so much to see.

CHAPTER 6 /

About my sister I can't say much with certainty. She was good at things that called for patience, such as drawing maps for school and colouring them in. When we were younger, I would watch if she let me when she brought home geography homework, admire the way she shaded in the countries with a pencil crayon held at a sharp angle to the paper, just so, never straying over a black borderline. When Katie filled the oceans, starting with a fringe of soft blue along the coasts, then moving evenly out to sea, it seemed perfect to me.

The way West Spirit Lake froze over at the beginning of every winter reminded me of Katie colouring in one of her maps. The ice also started at the edges and gradually moved toward the centre, out over the deepest part, strangling the open water. In the year of the sergeant, freeze-up didn't start until the middle of December, which was later than usual. It took a week to finally lock the lake up tight.

Between the morning when ice first appeared in the sheltered places along the shore and the evening when the channel was frozen clear across, things changed for me. The memory of those seven days comes easily and completely; I can move around in it and feel things again.

Freeze-up begins for real on a Sunday morning. My mother smokes her last Craven A at breakfast and sends me to the marina for a new supply. I haven't been spending as much time there as I like to since school began, and even less since hockey started, so I'm happy to head off running. A layer of snow only a few flakes deep has appeared overnight on the frozen ground, and I put the first tracks in it. When I reach the marina, before going inside, I walk out onto Babcock's dock. The rough boards are slick under my boots where the wave spray has turned to a hard glaze, and the lake beneath is frozen out as far as twenty feet from shore.

While I stand looking out at where the ice meets open water, Mr. Babcock's voice comes from behind me. "Your friend Julius was already here an hour ago, getting his boat gassed up."

"He's up early," I say, turning to face Mr. Babcock, but slowly so I don't slip.

"He got to town early for supplies. This is about the last day he'll want to try breaking through the shore ice with his little boat."

It was Julius's usual practice to hole up on White Dog Island during freeze-up. He would live alone with his dog until the ice was thick enough for him to risk taking his pickup across, at least six inches. After that, his driving back and forth would be a routine thing through the winter, and not at all dangerous, given the reliability of the ice through the cold months.

Mr. Babcock and I walk up to the marina together, talking about the weather and the water, which makes me feel like a man. As we step inside, Mrs. Babcock and Betty are sitting silently, side by side, on the old couch. Mrs. Babcock's head is lowered, creating triple chins. Betty is blowing on her first coffee of the day to cool it. As we pause in the doorway, my sense of the world I live in is, for a moment, perfectly concentric: at the middle is the dimple where Betty's breath hits the surface of her coffee, then come the ripples widening from that point, then the space around the couch where she sits, the marina, the town and the lake, the forest, and beyond, less distinct, everything else in the universe. Mrs. Babcock breaks this spell, raising herself up with a grunt and squeezing behind her counter, anticipating my request for cigarettes.

Betty says, "Look what blew in with the snow—a handsome stranger." Her voice is even raspier than usual at this early hour. "Long time no see. If I wasn't blinded by love, I'd suspect you were two-timing me."

She doesn't expect me to have a comeback for this, so she continues. "But I figure the new sergeant's keeping you too busy with your hockey for you to find time for running around after other females. At least, that's what I hear from your big sister."

This takes me by surprise, and Betty pauses to let it sink in. She has never mentioned Katie before, not once, and I can imagine no reason at all for the two of them to be talking about me, or, for that matter, anything else. Where would they meet? Why would they strike up a conversation? Katie never came to Babcock's Marina, and Betty, so far as I knew, rarely went anywhere else.

She must see the questions crossing my face, because she answers them. "Don't worry, my love, I don't have your sister spying on you. She was just over to the house the other night, shooting the breeze with my Annie, the way girls will, and I might have eavesdropped a little. That's a mother's right, after all."

Betty is not a boastful woman, exactly, but this information she passes along proudly. The upstanding daughter of the pharmacist has dropped over to socialize with her daughter—proof of some social standing. But the thought of Katie hanging around with Annie Peckford is only a little less surprising to me than the notion that my sister might somehow fall into an intimate chat with Betty herself. It's true that Annie is only two years older than Katie, but what could bring them together? Nothing I know about.

But, then, what I know about Annie is not much. That she has dropped out of school and works as a waitress at the coffee shop of the Blue Heron Motor Hotel, where her looks guarantee her

the biggest tips from the miners and highway construction workers who make up most of the clientele. That she has an older
brother, the one I once heard Betty refer to as a bad boy, and the
whole town knew he was in jail for a screwed-up attempt at rob-
bing the beer store.

Regarding Annie's father, I doubt anybody in town knew
much beyond the surname he had left behind. That he had
worked as a miner—the single most unsurprising piece of information one could obtain about a man in West Spirit Lake—could
not be forgotten, since Betty and her kids had been allowed to
stay on indefinitely in a mine house after he left town. That sort
of charity was expected of the company in a one-company town.

I give Betty's revelation no more response than a nod and a
shrug, and then run home faster than usual.

Katie is still munching toast when I hand our mother a new
pack of cigarettes to go with her third cup of coffee. I can't ask
my sister flat out about why she has paid a visit—more than one,
for all I know—to Annie Peckford. We didn't talk freely at that
time in our lives, and maybe we never really have or will. So I
need to find some other way to discover what is going on.

Katie doesn't leave the house the rest of that Sunday. It is one
of those odd days when the temperature drops steadily through
the sunlight hours—colder at noon than at dawn, and colder still
at dusk. Even when the sun breaks through, the water on the lake
looks more grey than blue. I don't think Katie realizes that I'm
keeping an eye on her. She spreads her homework out on the coffee table in the living room and works away at it with the TV on,
kneeling on the carpet, her posture perfect. The telephone rings
twice, and I jump to get it both times. For Katie, as usual, but it
is her regular friends calling, not Betty's Annie.

The next morning at school, something happens to push my
sister's double life to the back of my thoughts. A secretary from
the principal's office comes into our grade eight classroom just
before morning recess with a message for our teacher: I am to
go, along with Mike St. Vincent, to Mr. Kenison's office. I suffer
a moment of panic, as if I really am guilty of something, and then

anger when I think I must be implicated unjustly in something Mike has done.

But out in the hallway, before I can form the words to demand that he tell me what's up, Mike hisses at me, "What the hell did you do? Did you say I did something?"

When we get to the office, Mr. Kenison is not alone; Sgt. Martin is standing by his desk. Both are smiling. "Sit down, boys," Mr. Kenison says, and then, seeing us hesitating by the door, "Come on now, nothing to worry about."

"I was just telling Principal Kenison about how you boys pitch in over at the arena with the icemaking," Sgt. Martin says. "How'd you two like to take over while Julius is stuck over on his island? You'd get paid for it."

The sergeant proposes that during freeze-up, Mike and I get special permission to leave school an hour early every day to make sure the arena ice is ready for that evening's open skating and hockey. We would also have to stay late to scrape and flood the ice again at the end of the evening, before locking up the building. Our teacher would give us special dispensation regarding homework. And, of course, our parents would have to agree.

Mike looks as if an electric charge has gone through him. He thanks Sgt. Martin and Principal Kenison each several times, standing up and then sitting back down for no reason. In the hallway after we have been sent back to class, he raises his fists in the air and makes a silent cheer with his mouth wide open.

"We're out of this place early for at least a week," he says. "We're out of here. We're getting the keys to the arena. We've got the fucking run of the place."

"I don't know if my parents will let me," I lie.

He grins and says, "They will when the sergeant tells them to."

"Nobody tells my dad what to do, or my mom."

"The sergeant will."

He's got that right. By the time I'm home, my mother has been on the telephone with the principal's office and it is all arranged. "This is a big responsibility," Dad says at dinner. Mom adds, "Mr.

Kenison's putting a lot of trust in you." I notice she doesn't mention Sgt. Martin at all, even though this is obviously his idea.

Mike can't understand my lack of enthusiasm. He takes charge. The next day at school he watches the clock until the appointed time for our early exit. At exactly two-thirty, he closes the book on his desk with a thud and struts to the back of the room to pull on his coat and boots without even bothering to ask our teacher if it is okay to leave yet. I trail along behind him.

Strange to be walking through the streets at that hour on a weekday afternoon. No kids playing in the snow and few adults out and about. In the alleyway that we cut through on our way to the arena, a fat raven hops about on the ground, pecking at a frozen lump of garbage. As we get close, it flaps its wings twice to rise to the peak of the nearest garage roof and begins croaking at us, a brittle sound like a starter that's too weak to fire up a car engine in the cold. Looking down as I walk, I see the black bird's precise footprints in the snow, one repeated letter of a long-forgotten alphabet.

The clack-click of the lock sounds loud when Mike lets us in through the side door, and the arena seems more cavernous than usual. I stand by feeling useless as Mike gets to work. He wheels out the little tractor and floods the ice just as Julius has allowed him to a few times. I have never asked to try. Mike steers with one hand, glancing behind every few feet to monitor the flow of water, just as Julius does. It's a good job, and the ice will be true that evening.

By the time kids and coaches and parents arrive for the first hockey practice, Mike has everything in good shape. I haven't been much help. I follow him into Julius's little room under the bleachers, unsure what we should do now. Mike begins poking around Julius's things, first the tools, then leafing through the old man's books.

"Where the hell does he get these Polack books?"

"They're Latvian," I say. "Julius is always saying he's from Latvia."

This isn't strictly accurate. Julius only rarely volunteers information about his homeland and never any concerning his reading. Once or twice I asked him what the books were about, and his answers were peculiar. "Old man, old country, old books," went one short reply. "Old words," was an even briefer one.

Mike has never before shown any interest in the books. Now he flips through them as if he might somehow be able to decipher them. "Why don't you leave those alone," I say.

"Why don't you go fuck yourself," he shoots back.

I grab a push broom and go to sweep under the bleachers, a job I have done often enough for Julius. Crumpled coffee cups, chocolate bar wrappers, wads of pink gum frozen so they pop off the concrete in one piece when I scrape at them with a metal dustpan. I am sweeping when the sergeant arrives.

"Hard at it, eh?" he says. "Good lad. Where's your partner?"

I shrug. "No idea."

Sgt. Martin asks, "You two know you have to work as a team here, don't you?"

"Mike can probably do this job alone. Julius does most of the time."

He steps directly in front of my broom so I have to stop and look up at him. "That's not the attitude I'm expecting from you," he says. "Smarten up."

For a moment I am truly afraid. Then he exhales heavily and speaks with his mouth barely moving, so I have to listen hard to catch every word even in the muffled air under the bleachers.

"I'm going to tell you something. I know what kind of kid you are, what kind of family you're from, you and your sister. You're the kind of kids that will always get"—he pauses here to find the right words—"this sort of opportunity. Mike's not going to get a lot of these"—and again he takes a few beats for the correct phrase to come to him, touching the bottom fringe of his moustache with the tip of his tongue—"opportunities to show he can handle responsibility. You get me?"

I nod. But he's not finished.

"You have this job this week because you're a certain kind of young man. He's here because he's another kind. You'll get more breaks, don't worry. He might not. You going to screw this up for him?"

No adult has ever spoken to me like this before. He makes me feel a kind of burden that I have never felt, and, like something heavy in the trunk of a car driving on a slippery road, it gives me traction. The sergeant has inspired me, as he does our hockey team—there is no resisting it. I make up my mind in that moment to work hard and make sure there is peace between Mike and me.

And there is, for four days. We do a pretty good job together, with Mike still handling most of the important stuff.

Every morning of that week, though, I look out our kitchen window at the ice creeping in from all sides of the lake, anticipating the point when there will be no waves winking in the cold sunlight at the centre, and Julius can cross to take over the ice-making again.

That Friday night the arena is busier than usual. The local high school team, the West Spirit Lake Secondary School Prospectors, is playing a home game. I notice Katie, who doesn't always come to watch, sitting in the stands with some of her usual gang. I spot Annie Peckford, too, up behind the glass in the lobby, smoking with some older teenagers. And the sergeant is cruising around, as always, easy to pick out by his height. Once he gives the thumbs-up sign as Mike wheels out the tractor to get the ice in shape between periods.

After the game Mike and I sit together in the stands, waiting for the building to empty out so we can lock up. I see Katie's bunch walking to an exit, and then it hits me that she isn't with them. I jump up and go to check the lobby. Sure enough, there's my sister, talking with Annie, and the two of them are heading out together toward the parking lot.

I don't hesitate to follow. They pile into the back of an old car that I don't recognize. It already has three adult-looking silhouettes in its front seat, I can't make out exactly who. Then the car drives off, not in the direction of the heart of town, but out towards the highway. I stand for a moment, watching the red tail-lights disappear, and then set off running after it.

A lone boy trotting at a good pace through the winter darkness along the shoulder of a highway must be an odd sight. A few cars pass me, and one or two slow down to take a look. West Spirit Lake is small enough that I know I will be recognized. I don't care. As I run, I formulate a theory about where Katie and Annie are going. There are few possibilities, and my guess turns out to be right.

The Blue Heron Motor Hotel sits by the highway about a mile outside town. Once there was a Blue Heron Lodge, a four-storey hotel built during the gold rush days, but it burned down long before my family moved to West Spirit Lake. All I knew of the old place was a framed photo that hung behind the cash register of the namesake motel that replaced it. I liked the look of it, elegant in black and white.

Other than the name, however, the Blue Heron's two eras don't have much in common. The motel is about the same as any other motel, except that its bar, being the only drinking hole in a mining town, is a good deal busier than most. The neon sign in the window says Wading Bird Lounge, not a bad name, but everybody calls it the Dirty Bird.

I get a few curious stares from the drinkers as I stand in the doorway, panting a little from the run, and peering into the smoke. A waitress comes over. "What's up?" she asks.

"Nothing," I say. "I'm just looking for somebody."

"Look somewhere else," she says.

So I go to check the coffee shop, which is also pretty busy. I recognize quite a few high school kids, old enough to borrow their parents' cars to drive out after the game for fries and gravy. But Katie isn't among them. I give up and walk out into the motel parking lot under the red vacancy sign, and begin think about running back to town.

But a radio turned way up and mingled voices behind the music leak out into the cold. I bend down and scurry to take cover behind a parked pickup. Then, staying low, I edge along behind the row of cars and trucks, more than one per room, that line the front of the motel, over to where the noise is coming from.

Inside the room at least a dozen men and women perch on the edges of two double beds, or stand around, all holding beer bottles. The TV is on and a desk lamp, but no other lights, so it is shadowy. Still, I have no trouble making out several of them. First the new sergeant. He looks twice as big as anyone else, stretched out on a bed with his shoulders propped up against the headboard, at home. He appears immobile, or unmovable, and the other figures drift around him, around his room. Even his smile, under his moustache, looks fixed. There are some other adults I recognize, including a couple of cops and another two or three men I have seen working construction out on the highway as we drove past.

And then from the motel hall, or perhaps from the bathroom, Katie and Annie materialize. Somebody hands them each a beer. Katie takes a swallow. I have never seen this before. Watching, I swallow, too, but my mouth is dry.

Now I stand straight up, not caring to conceal myself anymore. But nobody notices me. So I step out from behind the car I have been crouching against, into full view in front of the room's big window. Still no reaction from those inside. Maybe they see only their own reflections when they look at the glass. That must be it. I feel as though I might float up into the night sky. I am about to bang on the door, except suddenly Katie is looking directly at me.

I wait for her to show some sign of recognition, shock at my being there, but after a few seconds she turns her face calmly away from me and goes back to talking close into Annie's ear. Katie has not been staring into my eyes, but into her own.

Next my sister makes another quarter-turn, this time away from Annie, so that her back is to the window. Her hair hangs a bit below the level horizon of her shoulders. (Dad is built like that, too—post and beam.) Somebody has said something to catch her attention. She walks over to the bed where the sergeant is stretched out. She hands him her beer and he takes a long drink, longer than anybody would ever need to, I think, before passing the bottle back to her. She takes a sip, not tilting her head the way he did, just tipping the bottle delicately to her lips. I can't look at this any longer.

The wind that had been at my back on the run out is in my face on the way home. I can feel my cheeks freezing but I don't care. My eyes are frosted half shut by the ice that forms on my lashes. When I get back to the arena, the lights are off, but Mike is waiting outside in the cold.

He asks, "Where the hell did you disappear to?"

"None of your business."

"No? I had to fucking close up by myself."

"Good for you. You can do the whole job alone until Julius gets back, as far as I'm concerned."

"As if I need you," Mike says. "What the hell's wrong with you? You crazy fucking fairy."

At that, I turn to walk home. Part of me wants to run, but I give in to another impulse—an unfamiliar one—which wants me to go as slowly as possible, never mind the cold.

When I finally arrive home, my parents are sitting together in the kitchen. I want to sit with them, maybe have a piece of toast before bed, and not talk about anything. But Dad says, "A little late tonight, aren't you?"

"Don't worry," I say. "I'm not going anymore. Mike or who-ever can handle the arena ice without me until Julius gets back."

"What, you two boys have a fight or something?"

"I'm just sick of it," I answer. "I've got better things to do."

In this moment I know that I don't want to be connected in anyone's mind with Mike St. Vincent anymore. It was the sergeant's idea to put us together. I am not his friend. I can't put any of this into words.

My father goes on talking. "You don't have to do anything you don't want to," he says, "but you do have to explain yourself to Prin-cipal Kenison and Sgt. Martin. They thought you'd be happy to help out at the arena, since you boys practically live there all winter."

"Yeah, well, that's going to change," I hear myself saying.

"Because I'm going to tell the sergeant that I'm quitting hockey, too."

It is the first I have thought of this and my own words take me by surprise.

"Quitting hockey? Hang on now . . ." my father starts, but my mother interrupts him. "Are you feeling all right?" she asks. "You look cold, or hot, or something." She presses her whole hand, palm and fingers, to my forehead. "Clammy," she says. "Off to bed."

So that's where I go, and I remain there all day Saturday. The thermometer shows that I am running a mild fever. Dad calls the sergeant and I hear him explaining that I'm not feeling well and won't be able to help out at the arena for at least a couple of days. He doesn't mention anything about me quitting hockey.

On Sunday, I make it out of bed but stay inside. I lie on the living room couch under a blanket for most of the day, but can't watch TV because Mom needs the piano in the living room to practise the pieces she'll be playing in the school Christmas show.

She has cajoled Katie into agreeing to accompany the youngest kids' choirs on a few pieces. When my sister comes into the room and sits beside my mother at the piano to play, I half-rise, thinking I will go back to my room and bed. I don't want to breathe the same air as her. But then I surrender, sink back down to listen, half-dozing. As my mother and sister discuss arrangements and take turns trying them out, I realize that with my eyes closed I cannot guess which of the two women in our family is playing at any given moment. They share a touch at the keyboard. Light but sure.

Sometime well after lunch my mother rises from the piano and goes over to the window to look out over the lake. Katie keeps playing "I Saw Three Ships Come Sailing In." I'm nearly asleep again. "It's frozen over," I hear my mother say. "I can't make out open water anymore."

That has the sound of good news to me. A relief. The end of freeze-up. The lake no longer so dangerous, both water and ice, part one thing, part another. Then I drop into a deeper sleep.

CHAPTER 7 /

To call up distinct recollections of any childhood Christmas is difficult. The real memories are silted over with images from photo albums and family slide shows. The people in the pictures age, but the objects carried up from the basement every year in cardboard boxes—candles made in grade two and never lit, red stockings fringed with fake white fur to hang from the mantle, balls for the tree nested in cartons like eggs—stay the same. They did what they were supposed to do: make every holiday like the one before.

But the Christmas when I was thirteen was different enough that I can peer past all that to what made it particular.

For one thing, I was sick. The fever that rose in me that night in early December when I ran out to the Blue Heron Motor Hotel and back turned into a chest cold that wouldn't go away. The doctor prescribed rest. Whatever was wrong with me concentrated itself at the point where, I imagined, my bronchial tubes divided. I had a distinct image of this piece of anatomy, an upside-down sling-shot shape, as it was shown on a garishly coloured poster of the parts of the body that hung on the wall of the examination room.

Through that whole winter, I could never quite cough that spot clear.

My hacking became an excuse for not returning to hockey. There was no need for a confrontation with the sergeant. I just couldn't play. I even managed, whenever I was asked about it, to look a little despondent about missing out on what was shaping up as a winning season.

I couldn't fool Mike, though. I felt his eyes on me when I returned to school after two dozy weeks at home. If my teacher asked about my health, I sensed Mike leaning forward an inch in his desk, waiting for my reply. "Much better," I'd say, but just mentioning it would prompt a cough or two. And even though the tickle in my throat was real enough, a tingle of guilt would pass through me. In these moments, I sometimes couldn't help glancing over my shoulder to the back of the classroom, and Mike would give me a look that fell somewhere between a knowing smile and a disgusted wince, before turning away.

In that year's Christmas photographs, I wear a turtleneck sweater, something my mother insisted on. I smile bravely. I have a hardcover book on my lap, a present, since I had lots of time to read. There is also a new chessboard on the coffee table, one of the folding kind designed for taking on trips; my father taught me to play between Boxing Day and New Year's, to take up some hours when I might in another year have been outdoors or at the arena. I hadn't known he had any interest in the game, but he turned out to be a good teacher. Katie didn't take it up. Like all those old decorations, she looks the same as always in that year's photos.

What comes back to me most, though, could never be captured by a camera. It was something hanging in the air, nothing thick, but there enough to be smelled and almost seen.

The medicinal presence of Vicks Vaporub was part of it. Both my parents swore by the ointment. My mother would dip two fingers into the cloudy jelly in the blue glass jar that was left on my dresser, then rub it on my chest before bed. In the middle of the night, if my coughing wouldn't let up, my father would sit me up in bed, pull my pajama top down off my shoulders, slather some on my back, and massage it in with a firmness that left no doubt this was, in his mind, a manly cure. Before turning out the light again, he would put a fresh dab of it by the steam vent on the vaporizer they plugged into the wall beside my bed each night. The room became so humid that a film of ice coated the inside of my window, changing the light during the daytime from ivory to mercury.

The something that was in the air of my room was in the sky above, too. On cold winter nights, the northern lights were always a possibility over West Spirit Lake, but the aurora borealis were never so common that anybody stopped marvelling at them. Except to me, that winter, when they showed themselves, the moving shapes seemed nothing out of the ordinary. Greenish white wisps, mauve swirls. One time a wide, pink band that expanded and contracted to an unsteady pulse. I looked up and saw these things, against the black and the stars, and thought, sure, that's how it is. I was groggy from medication and having trouble breathing through the clogged passages of my head and chest.

And it wasn't just the nighttime sky. Even on bright days—the coldest, without a trace of humidity—the blue above that season was like the blue of a very old person's eye. Walking to school one of those mornings in January, I saw two suns hanging over the horizon. This was also something to be expected up north: the sun and its sundog. Looking more closely, I made out that around the real sun was a pale ring, and saw how the second sun was like a diamond set in that ring.

When I arrived at school, I went right away to the library to ask Mrs. Lund about it. Since that day when she had told me about the two possibilities for how White Dog Island got its name, I had spent more and more time in her library, and sometimes found reasons to ask her for help looking things up.

"You want to know about sundogs now?" she asked. "Is this for a science project?"

"No," I said. "I just saw one this morning."

"Ah," she said. "Native curiosity. Let's go check the big book for a start."

The big book was what Mrs. Lund called the largest single-volume encyclopedia in her small collection, an old, fat, blue one with its spine curved in badly from being carried around open and dropped on the floor too often. It lay flat on a shelf by some atlases and dictionaries, from where she hoisted it down with her strong, skinny arms and laid it on a table.

"Sundog, sundog. . . . See parhelion. Parhelion, parhelion. . . . See halo. Well, that's helpful. Why didn't they say so in the first place? Now, let's see," she said. "Halley's comet, hallucination, Halmahera. . . . Here it is—halo."

We read the entry together until we came to the meaning we sought. A halo around the sun occurs when ice crystals in the atmosphere refract light. On this circle, mock suns appear sometimes. The big book said the same thing can happen with the moon. "I've never seen a moondog," I told Mrs. Lund.

"Look up more often," she advised.

"This is interesting," she went on. "It says here the theory of what causes mock suns, or sundogs, was first put forward by Descartes. Do you know who Descartes was?" I shook my head, so she told me. "He was the Frenchman who said, 'I think, therefore I am.' In Latin, '*cogito, ergo sum*'."

I asked, "What's that supposed to mean?"

"That's a harder one than 'What's a sundog?'" she said.

"But what's it mean?"

"It means," Mrs. Lund said, "it means the only thing you can't question is your own existence. Everything else is open to doubt."

"Like we doubt a sundog is really a sun," I said. "Might be just ice crystals."

"Smart guy," she said. "You can doubt something you see, but you can't doubt that you are really you."

I could see in her face and hear in her voice that she was enjoying this. So was I. I wanted to prolong our talk by thinking of something else to ask about Descartes and sundogs, what's real and what isn't. "But what if we're like the sun," I said slowly, not quite knowing where I was going. "What if you know you're real, okay, but there's another you, too, a fake you, and it can look just like you? Like a sundog."

"Hold on now, you're getting beyond what a mere librarian can look up for you," Mrs. Lund said without losing her smile.

"Whatever," I said. "Anyway, thanks for looking up sundog for me."

"You're very welcome," she said. "Any other atmospheric phenomena you'd like to explore today?"

"No thanks," I said. "If I need to, I can look in the encyclopedia myself. I better get to my class." I turned and started toward the door.

But Mrs. Lund didn't want to let go of me any more than I wanted to leave her and her big book. When I was a few strides away from the reference section, she said after me, "Just a sec. Do you really imagine that there's another you, an impersonator, out there?" She spoke in a normal voice, but it sounded loud in the library. We were the only ones there at that time in the morning.

"I don't know. Not exactly another me," I answered. "Maybe everybody has somebody who's just a little apart from them, who seems to belong with them, in a way, but not quite. Some people look at you, and look at somebody else, and think, 'Those two guys are sort of like each other,' but you're not really like each other at all. Not like you're related or something."

"That's a thought," Mrs. Lund said. "Maybe some of you students think I'm just like Mrs. Peterson"—the home economics teacher, who wasn't anything like Mrs. Lund—"because we're two ladies with Scandinavian names who've lost our husbands."

I hadn't given much thought to Mrs. Lund's existence beyond her library before. There was a moment of silence, but not an awkward moment. Mrs. Lund and I were just letting what she had said sink in, or drift off, respectful of each other's unspoken thoughts.

Then she said, "Don't be late for class, you." And I left.

I was never late for anything that winter. I was usually early. My cough was deemed bad enough that I shouldn't wait out in the schoolyard with the other kids for the bell to ring. So I came inside and read at my desk as soon as I arrived in the morning, stayed in most recesses, and headed home or to the drugstore immediately after school. For a while there was a certain novelty in my condition and my friends often said it was too bad. They would urge me to get better so I could come back to hockey. After a time they didn't bother mentioning it anymore.

Sgt. Martin asked only twice when I might be returning, and since both times I said nothing more than "I don't know," he stopped inquiring. It was beneath him to beg. Screw him, I thought. After the Christmas break, the team went back to winning games without me. But who cared? That's what I told myself, anyway.

Yet I found it harder than ever to keep my eyes off the new sergeant. The image of him in the motel room—lounging against the headboard of a double bed while the party went on around him—was not easy to reconcile with his public posture. When he was in school, which was often, I noticed how Principal Kenison walked a half-stride behind him in the hallway, hurrying but never quite catching up. Sgt. Martin's anti-vandalism campaign was being praised as a great success. (The fact that offenses had dropped off in the coldest months, when the nozzles of spray-paint cans froze up on about the second letter of a four-letter word, didn't seem to occur to anybody.)

I asked my parents if I could go to hockey games just to watch. Of course, they said, as long as I kept warm. So in early February, I started showing up at the arena again, sometimes helping out Julius a little, but mostly watching my old teammates from the lobby windows while a cherry cough drop dissolved on my tongue.

I noticed that things had changed. At the start of the season, Sgt. Martin had often shouted instructions at us during games. *Back check! Play the man!* Now, the guys knew what he wanted. He barely needed to part his lips. Arms crossed, he signalled the line changes with small gestures, lifting a gloved hand out of the folds of his coat sleeve. *You, on. You, sit this shift out. You, take a turn on defense.*

With Mike, he didn't need to do even that much. A flicker of eye contact and a quarter-inch movement of his chin were enough to send his star centre over the boards for a power play or to kill a penalty. That slight jerk of his face looked severe to me; I watched for it. If Mike was on the bench during a key moment of the game, he would keep glancing up to check the sergeant's reactions. So did most of the other players. They learned to read his features precisely.

Mike was still helping out Julius regularly, and this brought us into contact. The first time I returned to the icemaker's little room under the stands, Mike grunted, "Do you have to bring your fucking germs in here?"

Julius chuckled as if this were a light-hearted joke. He said, "Old man has lived under Nazis, Communists, now capitalists—germs are not so frightening." That was the first time I had heard him refer to politics. Mike looked at him funny and drew a slow circle with one finger in the air by his temple.

Once I asked Mike about how the team was doing. "I thought you were more interested in figure skating now," was his answer. Still, we sometimes scraped the ice together with shovels before Julius flooded it, or helped the old man haul his heavy hoses around. Julius welcomed me back into the routine as if I had never been gone, and, to make my recovery certain, urged me to drink weak tea with honey and take up eating yogourt.

Little things were different in the icemaker's room. In the few weeks that I was laid up, Mike had begun drinking the coffee from Julius's thermos without asking, pouring himself some into a Styrofoam cup he had taken to keeping on a shelf in the little room, and sometimes filling Julius's broken china one while he was at it. Seeing this new familiarity between them made me feel like an outsider.

Being back around the arena let me keep an eye on Katie, too. She was often there, always with the same school friends, though never, as far as I could see, with Annie Peckford. Maybe, I began to think, their ride together out to the Blue Heron had been a one-time-only thing. Maybe when Katie looked into her own eyes reflected in the motel room window that night, she saw how wrong it was to be there, with the new sergeant's legs stretched out and crossed at the ankles on the double bed right behind her. Wrong to give him that swig of beer and then take one herself. I didn't dare ask her, didn't know how. As the weeks passed, the urgency of my desire to find out what she had been doing there dulled. I had found a way to stay a little apart from things, including those unanswered questions.

Then, early one Saturday morning in February, the slow rhythm I was slipping into was jolted. I was lying in bed, looking at the vertical bar of light on my wall, created by the sun breaking through the gap between my curtains, when my mother tapped on my door. "There's somebody here to see you," she said.

"Who?" I asked.

"One of the boys from hockey," she said. "Michel." It took me a beat to realize she meant Mike.

I didn't want him to see me in my pajamas, so I pulled on jeans and a sweatshirt over top of them. He was standing inside the kitchen door.

"Come on," he said.

"Come on where?" I asked.

"Come on with me."

Something about the level way he said this, the way he didn't blink as he looked straight at me, made me obey. I told my mother that I was going up to the arena. She seemed to find Mike's seriousness amusing. "You go on," she said. "I can see you boys have business to attend to." I had made up the bit about the arena, but it turned out to be true. Mike headed in that direction with me behind him. "What's going on?" I asked.

"You'll see," was all he would say, and I couldn't be sure if he was happy or sad or angry, only that he was excited.

We entered the arena through Julius's side door, which was unlocked. Mike had evidently already been there. He strode straight to the little room under the stands, and stood pointing under the rough carpenter's table on which Julius often drank his coffee and repaired and oiled his icemaking gear. We had walked in so quickly that my eyes were still adjusting from the brightness of the morning to the gloom of the interior, so it took me a minute, peering under the table, to see what was back there.

It was a small safe, blue and silver. It reminded me of an old-fashioned Christmas ornament, except much more solid, resting heavily on the concrete floor as if it might always have been there. But it hadn't. Mike and I knew the room well—every old calendar, every shovel and broom, file and wrench, hung on a nail in its assigned place on the wall. Julius's big, red tool box had been rolled aside from its usual position under the table to reveal the safe. Otherwise, the new, foreign thing would have been hidden behind it.

I asked, "How'd you find it?"

"When I came in this morning, Julius was looking at it," Mike said. "Just sitting here, sort of mumbling, looking at it."

"So where'd it come from?" I asked.

"Fucked if I know," Mike said.

"What's Julius say?"

"Ask him yourself," he said. "He's up in the stands."

Julius was holding his old cup but not drinking, gazing out at nothing over the surface of his ice. He had turned on all the lights, and the mist around them did not stir. He was hunched over even more than usual, a little curl of a man, under the massive curvature of the wooden rafters. He looked terribly small, a scrap of something left behind in an unpacked crate. Mike and I clambered up and took our seats on either side of him.

"Julius," I said. "Where did the little safe come from?"

"Don't ask the old man," he replied.

"Is it yours?" I asked.

"Does an old man need a strongbox?" he said.

The word *strongbox* sounded like something from a late-night movie to me. That's what it is, I thought, a strongbox. Julius's voice was tired, as if he had hauled the heavy thing himself into his little sanctuary.

I tried another way. "Okay, who does need a strongbox?"

Now he looked at me sadly. "Who needs? Who needs?

Everybody knows the answer to this. Who has," he said. "Who has something to put in. The rich. The authorities."

I had never before heard Julius mention anything about "the rich." But "the authorities"—that had a familiar ring to it. Wasn't that what he had once called the new sergeant?

"You mean Sgt. Martin?" I said, taking a stab. "Is that whose safe it is?"

With pain in every line on his face, Julius looked first at me, then up at the fog hanging still around the arena lights. "Don't ask the old man." I thought he might shed tears. "Please, boy."

"Just shake your head if I'm wrong," I said.

"Please, you're a good boy, don't ask the old man."

Mike and I went back to the room. We both crouched down on our haunches to get a good look at the safe. In the shadow under the table, its metal had a dull gleam and its blue trim was vivid. "What's all that shit about the sergeant?" Mike asked. "You figure this is his?"

"It's his," I said.

"How the hell can you know that?" Mike demanded. But in his tone there was respect for what I had deduced. "I mean, how the fuck can you figure from what Julius said that it's the sergeant's?"

"Think about it," I said. "Who else is around here all the time? Who comes down to Julius's room, other than us? Anyway, Julius said something before about the authorities. That's what he calls the cops. That's who he said needs a safe."

Mike mulled this over. "Sgt. Martin's got to have a reason for bringing that thing here," he said. "It must be cop business."

"If it was cop business, they'd have it down at the station," I said. "Anyhow, Sgt. Martin's not a regular cop."

"What do you mean, he's not a regular cop?"

"I mean, when he came here, remember they said maybe this was his punishment, West Spirit Lake, for whatever he did wrong somewhere else." I wanted to tell him about the motel party, but what was there to tell exactly? So I added only, "And there's other stuff I know about that I can't tell you."

"You know fuck all," Mike challenged me.

At that, I had to say something. "You know that night I ran out of here? I ran all the way to the Blue Heron. The sergeant's living out there. He was having a party in his room—I saw—and it was no cop party. It looked like"—now I had to improvise— "dope dealers, maybe, and whores." A word I had never spoken.

I half expected Mike to call me a liar, but he didn't. Instead, he accepted what I had described and put his own spin on it. "There's no real dope dealers in West Spirit," he said. "I know from the guys at the rec hall. The only thing happening in this shit-hole town is high-grading from the mine."

We looked at each other for two silent seconds, then at the safe again, as if we might see through the metal. What if the talk Mike had heard over the pool tables was right? What if somebody was smuggling gold out of the mine? Could it be the sergeant was in on it? Maybe the strongbox was full of chunks of raw high-grade, embedded in white quartz veins, carried past the gates of the West Spirit Lake Gold Co. Ltd. in body cavities and the hollowed-out heels of workboots and lunch buckets rigged with false bottoms. We all had heard the stories. I even knew how the gold would look—not sparkly like the pyrite kids collected from the crushed rock dumped around the mine site as waste, but a dull, buttery yellow.

Mike broke the silence. "What are we going to do?"

I didn't have an answer. I was thinking about gold, and about how I had said to Mike that there were whores at the sergeant's party. That was just to get his attention, I told myself, like saying there were drug dealers there. I hadn't meant it.

"What the fuck are we going to do?" he repeated.

"We know this safe is the sergeant's," I said. "We find out what he's up to. We watch him. If he's buying high-grade, then we turn him in—we go to the old sergeant."

"Then maybe we get a reward or something," Mike said. "But I doubt it. I still say the new sergeant's not the type. This safe is probably cop business. "

We then hatched a plan to watch Sgt. Martin. I knew which

room he had out at the motel. Mike said he could go out there and keep an eye on it some nights; his parents would never know. He didn't press me on what exactly I was going to contribute to our scheme. He took it for granted that we were in this together.

"What about Julius?" I asked.

"He's scared shitless," Mike said. "He's not telling nobody nothing."

When we left the little room, Julius was no longer in the bleachers. They were empty. The lights were off. His pickup was gone from the arena parking lot. He must have headed home to his island. I walked back through town with Mike to his house. We didn't talk much more. It was still early, and the dogs that noticed us passing were barking their first barks of the day.

The town seemed very low to the earth that morning, as if it was hunkering down for warmth. When they built houses for the miners at West Spirit Lake, back in the gold rush days, they bull-dozed the forest. Topsoil is thin over the rock in the country north of Lake Superior, so the trees did not grow back very well. Some of the yards had clumps of birches, four or five delicate trunks from a single root, and some miners' wives had trans-planted mountain ashes from the nearby bush for the berries that cling all winter and attract birds. But these were not tall, not even reaching to the peaks of the little bungalows.

As we walked, Mike looked down, kicking along a ball of dirty snow until it broke apart, and then using his heel to knock loose another hard-packed clump from the base of the shoulder-high snowbanks that lined the streets, left behind by the road ploughs. His feet stayed busy this way and his eyes had something to follow.

I was gazing at the housetops, noticing how the smoke from the chimneys came out almost horizontally, following the line of the roofs, the way it does when it is very cold. I wondered why that was, and thought that on Monday I would go see if Mrs. Lund could find me the reason in her library. It was nice, for a moment, to stop wondering about what was in that safe, about the motel, about what was happening in West Spirit Lake, and think only about answers that might come from a book.

CHAPTER 8/

S o I gave up trying not to be paired with Mike. It was a relief. It took less energy. We started speaking regularly before class was let in, usually meeting outside in a narrow space where the white-shingled wall of the school was only three feet from the chain-link fence that surrounded it. This passageway was hidden enough that kids could smoke there without much chance of being seen by a teacher. I would arrive a minute or two before Mike most mornings, and grew accustomed to watching him light up, shielding his match expertly against the wind, chin down, hands cupped, letting the flame gain just enough independence before he exposed it to the tip of his cigarette, then inhaling no more than was needed to make an ember.

That was one of the things he did very well; another was lacing up his skates fast and tight. But he was a lousy student, except that he rarely made a mistake on a spelling quiz. And on the multiplication tables—two times two through twelve times twelve—he never even hesitated. If the way something had to be done was dead certain, no room for argument, that's how he did it.

He wasted no time figuring out a way to watch Sgt. Martin. On the first Monday after we discovered the safe, he caught a ride out to the Blue Heron in the early evening with one of the older snooker players from the rec hall. First Mike ate a plate of French fries at the motel coffee shop, and then he slipped out to keep watch on the room. (I had told him which door was the sergeant's—nine—easy to remember because it was by convention the sweater number of the highest-scoring hockey stars.) The lights were out, the curtains drawn. After quite a while, maybe an hour Mike later told me, the sergeant pulled up in a cruiser, alone, and went inside to change out of uniform. Then he went to the coffee shop for dinner.

"Did you see if he ate with anybody?" I interrupted when Mike was recounting all this the next morning.

"No, he ate at the counter," he said. "I could see him the whole time from the pinball machine in the hall by the cash register."

That was a smart place to watch from. "He talk to anybody?"

"The waitress, Annie what's-her-name," Mike said, then added with a smirk, "Your girlfriend's daughter."

It had been some time since Mike had mocked me about old Betty. The sting had gone out of it, if there was ever much to begin with. In fact, I had been spending so little time down at the marina lately that I hardly saw the old fortune teller anymore. Anyway, I let it pass.

"Talking to the waitress doesn't count," I said.

"Annie wasn't just refilling his coffee," Mike said. "She kept coming back and talking to him all the time. You know, friendly."

Of course, this wasn't a complete surprise to me. I felt I had to let Mike in on a little more about what I had seen at the sergeant's party, although there was no reason to mention Katie. "You know that party I told you about, when I saw into the sergeant's room," I said. "Annie Peckford was there."

"Holy shit," Mike said. "She's barely older than us. She's probably screwing him."

I didn't like to hear him jump to that conclusion out loud, and I felt like firing back, That's not true, there were lots of people in the room, it was a party. But all I said was, "Even if she is, what's that got to do with the safe?"

To this Mike pulled his shoulders up in the first half of a shrug as he took a final drag on his cigarette. He flicked the filter end into the snow. Perfect timing. The bell rang, he let his shoulders drop to complete the gesture, exhaling smoke, and with that we headed inside with the rest of the kids.

From then on Mike went out to the Blue Heron as often as he could, two or three times a week through February. He made the pinball machine in the motel lobby his excuse, and told me he was getting good at it, but his snooker game was suffering from neglect. Sgt. Martin got used to seeing him there, and sometimes asked Mike if he didn't have a home to go to. But the sergeant didn't seem seriously concerned about Mike's hanging around. Mike was the sort of kid who could get away with stuff like that; somebody would have called my parents.

One evening, the sergeant even stopped on his way into the coffee shop for dinner to watch Mike play three balls. "He said he liked pinball when he was a kid, and then we talked hockey for a while," Mike told me. "He's basically a good guy. I'm thinking maybe the safe is cop business, totally legitimate."

"Basically a good guy," I said. "Right."

"What's that supposed to mean?" Mike said. "What shit. What've you got against him, anyway?"

It was the first time Mike had openly defended Sgt. Martin since we made the discovery in Julius's little room. "I've got nothing against him," I said. "I'm just trying to figure stuff out, like you."

"Like hell," Mike said. "You want to nail him. I just want to know about the safe."

"Same thing," I said. Then I decided to change the subject. "He still talking all the time to Annie?"

"Practically between every bite. They're definitely doing it."

"But you never see her go to his room, right?"

"I never *see* her go," Mike admitted. "But all I can watch is the outside door, and only sometimes. Why would she go outside?

There's the inside hallway. And once she's in his room, the curtains are always closed."

We weren't getting far. Without much to talk about from Mike's reconnaissance, our morning conversations broadened. "You still hiding out in trash cans from your dad?" I risked asking one morning.

"He's onto that one," Mike said, laughing. "But I've got a better spot—up in the rafters of the garage. The other day, he came in poking around and stood right fucking under me. I think he knew I was there somewhere but he's too dumb to look up. I was afraid to take a fucking breath."

"He'll look up someday," I said. "You'd better not keep hiding there."

Mike frowned to show he was giving my advice serious thought. "Maybe," he finally said. "But when he's drinking, he's pretty stupid. He might never catch on. Anyway, I'm not so worried if he sees me."

"What happens then?" I asked, though I wasn't sure that I wanted to know.

"Not too much. He's thinking twice these days about whacking me. I beat him in arm wrestling almost all the time now. He says he lets me win, but I know he knows I can take him any fucking time."

I didn't doubt it.

Mike asked me things, too, though hesitantly. "Your old man, he must make a mint with that store," he said out of the blue one day.

"Not that much," I said.

"Come on, look at the car you guys got," Mike said. "Look at your boat." The way he said it was not like he thought we didn't deserve a nice car and boat, just that he admired them.

"I guess they're okay," I allowed. "The boat's cool. Next summer, I'm getting water skis." Mike nodded a few times slowly and blew out smoke evenly as he considered the idea of water skiing.

Then he said something that surprised me. "I can't swim."

Everybody in West Spirit Lake could swim. I had never met a kid who couldn't. The shoreline was part of the town. I didn't know what to say without sounding like I was making fun of him, so I didn't say anything. Mike filled in the silence.

"The town where we lived before we came here didn't have a lake," he said. "Just a river that smelled worse than shit from the paper mill. That's where my dad worked before. He says he likes hard rock mining better than mill work, because at least underground it doesn't stink, it's clean."

The idea that drilling and blasting and mucking out the stopes deep beneath the West Spirit Lake Gold Co. Ltd. headframe was clean work was a new one to me. It made me think about my father in his white jacket at the back of his pharmacy. I wondered what Mr. St. Vincent would say about a man whose workday was spent counting out pills on a spotless surface, moving them into little piles with a new wooden tongue depressor, weighing out powders on a stainless steel scale.

But Mike was still thinking about swimming, not our fathers' jobs. "I'm not afraid of water," he said. "I just never learned to swim."

"You can learn this summer," I said. "There's lessons at the beach."

"Like I'm going to take dog-paddling lessons with babies," he scoffed.

"Well, there's the sandbar in the river," I said. "Nobody goes up that way much. It's colder than the lake, but it's shallow. You could teach yourself there."

"What the hell," Mike said. "We'll check it out. Worst thing that happens is you get to watch me drown."

So we had decided, huddling against the school wall in the late February cold, to go swimming together that summer.

Around that time my mother asked me one night if we could have a talk. She was so solemn that for a moment I thought somehow she knew about the safe, how we were watching the sergeant, the whole thing. "I know I'm not such a good influence on you in this area," she started. "But you know we can't have you smoking. It's terrible for your health, especially with this bad cough you've had."

I might have laughed out loud if she hadn't looked so worried. "I'm not smoking," I said. "Honest. Not one drag."

"Honey," she said. "Be sure you're telling the truth. I smell it every day on your coat. Your father has noticed it, too."

"That's not me," I explained. "That's one of the guys at school. He's smoking half the time I'm around him. What can I do?"

By the way she relaxed her shoulders I could see she believed me. "Well, that's a relief—I thought I was going to have to quit to get you to," she laughed. "Who is this young nicotine slave? That boy Michel who came to fetch you out of bed a few Saturday mornings back?"

"Mike, he's called Mike," I said. "Why do you guess it's him?"

"He's got the look," she said. "A little rough around the edges, like your old mother. So is Michel a big pal of yours these days?"

I wasn't sure how to answer this question, so I left it hanging. Mom said, "That's okay. As long as you don't take up cigarettes to go along with him. To thine own self be true."

She used to say that all the time, and it was never clear to me how much she intended it as a joke. On this occasion, though, I took it that she meant it, and afterwards whenever she tossed it out, the motto always brought back a thought of Mike and me at that time, and what it might mean to be true to oneself.

After Mike had been diligently haunting the Blue Heron for a few weeks, I started feeling that I should be contributing something to our—what was it? Spying? No. That made it sound like a kids' game, as if it was part of the world of riding bikes up to the airport to watch the gold being loaded on a plane. An investigation? Worse. Too big. I could hear my father using the word with amusement if he discovered what we were up to. "So, you two sleuths launched your own investigation. . . ."

Whatever it was, I had to do more than listen to Mike's morning reports. There was no way for me to go out to the Blue Heron without attracting attention. That would have to remain Mike's end. But I couldn't stop pondering his theory about Sgt. Martin and Annie Peckford. Sure, it could be. And I might be able to confirm it, or at least gather more evidence—if I could somehow get Betty to reveal something without her ever knowing what I was after. Anything about her daughter's life. A clue. I decided to head down to Babcock's to try.

I hadn't been at the marina much during those winter months. So when I stepped into the cluttered shop on the morning of the first Saturday in March, I felt a little self-conscious.

As usual, Mrs. Babcock was installed behind her glass-topped counter. "Smokes for your mum?" she asked me.

"No thanks," I said, looking around for something to occupy myself.

She went back to peeling the little plastic liners out of bottle caps, a pile of which was growing on her counter. I had seen her at this task often before. Most of the liners said TRY AGAIN but a few were good for a prize from the bottler, if you collected enough, or at least entitled you to enter a grand prize draw. Retailers were forbidden from winning these contests, but the Babcocks regularly collected all the caps discarded in the oil can beside their Coke machine, sorted them, and then had an accomplice claim the booty and split the proceeds.

Betty's couch was empty. And then, looking around, I realized from the stuff piled up on the stained cushions—cardboard boxes of Lifesavers and chocolate bars waiting to be stocked, bundles of hunting and fishing magazines—that nobody had been sitting there lately.

I wanted to ask where Betty was, but that would have been too blunt an admission of interest. After a minute or two I realized that standing around not buying anything and hoping she came in weren't going to work, either. I decided to hunt elsewhere for information. "Is Mr. Babcock around today?" I asked.

"Out in the shop," Mrs. Babcock said, peering at me more closely. "He might need a hand, I guess."

So I wandered back to the shed. It felt colder in there than outside. The plank walls were bare of insulation other than some plastic sheeting stapled up to keep the wind from slicing through the cracks. The coils of two electric space heaters glowed orange, one on either side of Mr. Babcock, as he leaned over the exposed engine of a Ski-Doo. He scowled at me for bringing in a gust of the late winter air.

"God damn these damn Bombardiers," he said by way of a greeting, pronouncing it Bom-ba-DEERS, as everybody but the French Canadians did around West Spirit Lake. "God damn these damn two-cylinder shit boxes."

I peered down into the engine while he fiddled with the carburetor. Even with the two heaters burning away, his hands looked numb. The light wasn't good, either, so I picked up the flashlight from his bench and shined it on his greasy fingers. He made the adjustment he wanted, and then tugged the pull-cord to start up the engine. The noise shook the whole hut and rattled every wrench and screwdriver that hung on its walls. Mr. Babcock looked satisfied. After letting the engine settle into a coughing idle for a minute, he shut it off. In the quiet that followed, we both watched the blue exhaust smoke hanging in the shaft of morning sunlight that came in through the shed's solitary square window.

"You got another machine to work on?" I asked.

"In a bit," he said. "I better warm my damn fingers up first." His hands were jammed down into his pockets. Over his coveralls he was wearing a red flannel shirt and over that an oily, orange hunter's vest.

As we were sitting motionless anyway, I hoped my question would sound like nothing more than passing the time. "Where's Betty?" I asked. "I stuck my head in the store and Mrs. Babcock was on her own for once."

Mr. Babcock pulled his hands out of his pockets to see if putting them up under his arms was any better. "Betty's not around here so much these days," he said. "It's cold walking all the way from the townsite down here to the lake this miserable time of year."

"Since when does Betty give a damn about the weather?" I asked him. I had seen her trudging to the marina through rain with nothing to keep her head dry but a baseball cap. In deep snow, all she wore on her feet was a pair of steel-toed miner's workboots lined with nothing thicker than grey wool socks, which she pulled up out of the boots and over the cuffs of her pants.

Mr. Babcock pulled his hands out from under his arms, cupped them, and breathed heavily, *haah*, into them. "I guess she doesn't give a damn," he conceded. Then Mr. Babcock glanced at me, and back again at the smoke hanging in the light, and finally he began to speak.

"You know Betty's daughter Annie? Now, that girl means everything to her, and I mean every damn thing. She sees her younger self. I know Betty is a sorry sight now, but she was a good-looking female in her day."

He shot a look at me now as though I might challenge him on this improbable claim. But I wasn't about to interrupt, and anyway I believed him, so he went on.

"And her day wasn't so long ago, you know. I wouldn't think she's fifty-five yet. But every year has been like two since Frank Peckford ran off on her. You wouldn't remember him, would you?"

No, I wouldn't. In fact, I hadn't been born when Annie's father left West Spirit Lake. But I didn't bother pointing that out to Mr. Babcock. I just shook my head.

"Well, Frank was a piece of work. Not that I remember all that much about him anyway. Leave the gossip to the women, god-damn it. He was from Newfoundland and Betty's people are from Cape Breton. Betty used to say back then, 'Frank dances and I sing, and between us we'll have a hell of a time and no money.' Anyway, he stayed on ten years—that's not so long as you think, you'll find that out someday—and then left her with the two kids."

He fell silent for a spell but I knew he wasn't finished. This was the longest I had heard Mr. Babcock go on since the day he told me about Betty's gift for interpreting melodies to tell the future. There was something about her that made him talk. I wondered what he himself had been like in those old days he spoke of now, back before Betty's teeth had gone bad, when he and Mrs. Babcock, after all, were also young. I wondered if maybe they had danced and drank beer together, the four of them around a table at the Blue Heron, in all its old four-storey glory, before it had burned down and been replaced by the motel out on the highway.

"Betty's two kids," he picked up where he had left off. "You've heard about the boy, I guess. He'll be in deluxe accommodations at the Stony Mountain Inn out in Manitoba for a few more years yet. When they let him out, let's hope he doesn't come back this way. Betty doesn't need that. No sir. Her girl, Annie—there's some hope for her. But Betty worries the daughter is going the son's way now, or the father's, or whatever. She's a mother—it's breaking her heart."

"Is that why she's not hanging around here much lately?" I asked.

"I would say," he nodded. And then he added, "Betty thought maybe your big sister would be a good influence on her Annie. Better class of friend, you know, or some goddamn thing. But I guess that hasn't done the trick."

He stepped over to his workbench and picked up one greasy spark plug, then another. He held them both up to the light of the little window and squinted at them. The snowmobile exhaust had dissipated while he was speaking; the air was now clear in the shaft of light. He pulled out a jackknife and started scraping carbon off the plugs with a small blade. Definitely a one-man job. I turned and went out while he attended to this close work.

I did not run home but walked. On the way I decided that I must speak finally with Katie.

I found her in her room. It was not a typical teenager's refuge. She had a record player, a gift from our grandparents, but rarely played music. The LPs my parents sometimes gave her on her birthday or Christmas—a natural present for a girl so musical—were leaned very neatly on a shelf beside the turntable. She had plenty of books as well, and they were also tidily shelved. Nothing was tacked to the walls.

When I tapped on her open door and stepped in, she said, "Oh, it's you," as if she might have been expecting somebody else. She was lying on her bed, on top of the flat spread, staring at the ceiling and toying with a bracelet. It was an old-fashioned silver one my mother had given her years before. When she first started wearing it, it dangled loose on her wrist, looking as though it might fall off if she didn't keep her thumb out, and back then she could easily slide it up her arm past her elbow. Now I noticed that her arms looked strong, like our father's, and the bracelet would slip up no further than her forearm.

"Can I talk to you?" I asked.

"Can it wait?" she said, mocking me by imitating the cadence of my question. I came in anyway and sat on her desk chair, my only option aside from the edge of her bed, which was out of the question.

"Katie," I started, and just saying her name out loud reinforced the awkward way I was going at this. "Look, I was out at the Blue Heron a few weeks ago, last month I guess, and I saw you at a party or something."

She might have tensed for a second as though about to sit up suddenly, but she remained lying flat. She put one hand over each eye, as if what I had said changed the view of the blank ceiling above her to something she couldn't stand the sight of. With her eyes covered, I found myself concentrating on her lips as she spoke: "Why do you care what I do? It's none of your business. What were you doing out there anyway?"

She sounded so tired. Not angry. Much older.

"I don't know," I said. "There's something going on. The new sergeant, Sgt. Martin, he's into something. I can't tell you everything. But he's maybe going to be in trouble. You remember what Mr. Brascomb said—why does he live way out there at the motel anyway? Why doesn't he live in town?"

"He lives out there because you can't move, you can't budge an inch, in West Spirit without everybody knowing every little thing," she said. "God, aren't you sick of this place, too? I mean, you don't even have hockey anymore. I see you at school, you know. You used to have friends, at least. Now you never hang out with anybody except that new kid."

"What new kid?"

"You know—that new kid, Mike St. Whatever. You're always talking to him when he's having a smoke."

It had never occurred to me that Katie noticed anything I did. She never let on. The high school was next door but set apart from the public school. It seemed remote. She and her friends moved on a different plane, and I could look up at her and them, but she could never look down at me. My mind spun back to those months when I was being picked on in kindergarten, and Katie had urged me to endure. She had been watching then, too.

"Remember when we lived in the trailer the first year here?" I said. "Remember that kid who drowned?"

"Sure," Katie said. "He had two sisters. They moved away."

"The next year," I said. "Exactly a year later. I remember. It was breakup time again when the moving van came."

"What about them?" she asked.

"Nothing."

"You were all screwed up over that kid Alvin drowning," she said.

"I guess," I said. "I was little."

"You all screwed up again now?"

"No. Not really," I said. "All I'm saying is, I saw you at the Blue Heron at some kind of party with the new sergeant. And I'm telling you, there's something wrong with that guy."

Katie rolled over onto her side to look at me and put her two hands, palm to palm, under the side of her face. This was the pose she used to strike when she was little and pretending to be asleep to try to trick my parents. Except now her eyes were wide open, not squeezed shut, and she was sizing me up.

"Are you going to start looking out for me now?" she said, kind of teasing, kind of making me feel good.

"Remember the fort?" I asked. "I wonder if it's still there, and those pots and pans we used to play with."

"Those pots and pans were already rusting away when we were little," she said. "But maybe the fort is still there if new kids kept fixing it up like we did. You can always nail up new boards."

The thought of generations of trailor kids keeping the tree house in good repair made me feel better. "Do you know anything about the sergeant?" I pressed. "Has he got a lot of money, like more money than a cop should have, do you think?"

"How much money should a cop have?" she said. "Look, detective, I've been out to his room a couple times. People go there to drink beer and listen to the radio and watch TV and stuff. It's no big deal."

I nearly asked her since when did she drink beer, but that would have ruined everything. Unbidden, the thought crossed my mind that the sergeant must have drained half her bottle in that one long pull he took. For a minute more I sat in her chair silently, the image of that bottle emptying in my head, while Katie lay on her side, looking at me with sleepy eyes, or weary ones. Then it seemed I should go. When I stood up and went next door to my own room, and stretched out on my own bed, I listened hard for any sound through the wall of Katie moving around. Nothing.

Yet she must have slipped out quietly, because when I roused myself a while later to find some lunch, she was no longer in. Mom said she had headed out to meet some friends and wouldn't be back until after supper. When I heard that, loneliness coursed through me in an instant, like a poison, as if she had gone away for good.

CHAPTER 9/

A few days after my talk with Katie, I stood in the alley behind Betty Peckford's house. It was another cold morning, but now that March had come, the winter's bone-white sun was yellowing, and its light carried enough heat to raise just a trace of moisture from the packed snow. The sound my boots made had changed from a squeak to a crunch. I walked up to Betty's back gate as noiselessly as I could to avoid rousing her dog, a husky called Curly, not after his hair, which was straight and white and thick, but for the feathery tail that curled up over his back like a question mark.

Betty's dog never barked, which was taken by some kids as an indication of sneakiness and a potential to bite. (In a town where private property didn't count for much and kids made shortcuts through whatever yards they pleased, it was important to know the temperaments of the resident dogs.) But I tended to think that Curly was not a danger, perhaps even gentle, based on some odd behaviour I had witnessed from him.

What I saw happened on a sweltering summer day, when Betty had brought Curly down to Babcock's Marina. This was not the usual thing, but that afternoon Betty said she thought the poor animal might need a swim. While Betty was inside, I noticed Curly stalking some small creature in the wet grass by the water's edge, looking more cat than dog. I edged closer to see what he was hunting, and saw that it was a tiny leopard frog.

As I stood nearby and watched, Curly pounced, caught the frog under a paw, opened his pink mouth and seemed to neatly gobble it up. My stomach turned but I couldn't look away. Then Curly spread his jaws again, as if yawning—and the frog hopped out. This game was repeated a couple of times more before the frog finally managed to jump beyond the shore grass to the shallow water and swim off. Curly stood as still as a wading bird, in water halfway up his legs, scanning the sparkling surface, moving just his eyes, his head motionless, as if he might take up the pursuit again whenever his prey came up for air. But the frog outlasted him. After a while Curly sauntered off to lie panting on the gravel by the marina door and wait for Betty to emerge and head for home.

So on that March morning, with the frog episode in mind, I supposed it was safe to walk up to Betty's back door even with Curly keeping guard on the concrete steps. As well, I supposed that my sister Katie must have walked through this yard more than once. Curly looked snug in his white pelt, and I imagined he might be put in a good mood by the sun, even though a breeze was ruffling the hair on his shoulders. Huskies like Curly were West Spirit Lake's most common breed, wolfish around the jaws and in their gait. But I told myself they were bred for hauling, not to be mean.

I opened the gate. At the click of the latch Curly rose, rear end first, had a nice stretch with his front paws down, and then came to meet me halfway up the walk, wagging his spiral tail. He licked my mitten with the tongue that the frog had used as a diving board, and stayed at my heels as I tapped on the door. I felt silly for having spent even a minute worrying about how he might react to me. Betty didn't answer right away, so I had time to survey the yard. Curly's doghouse, unpainted. A pile of firewood, mostly birch, which burns nice and slow. On two sawhorses, a canoe, the old kind of stretched red canvas, patched and in need of more patching. Yellow marks in the snow over by the fence where Curly went, and a faint sour smell that would sharpen when the true spring melt came in a month or so.

I was beginning to think nobody was home when the door behind me opened. Betty was dressed as she generally was at Babcock's, in jeans and a heavy shirt, except that now she also wore plaid carpet slippers. They were the kind my grandmother favoured; I took note of the hole worn through the toe of one before raising my eyes to her face. Betty made an almost inaudible whistling sound, three short notes, in the cadence of *well, well, well.*

"I'm looking for Katie," I said. It was the excuse I had thought up in advance. "I figured she might be here maybe visiting Annie."

In fact, Katie had been at home taking her time over breakfast when I bustled out. She would have no reason to notice that I was in a hurry—I often was when I had to be at the arena early to help out Julius on a weekend morning.

Beyond my idea of using the ruse of looking for my sister, I had no idea of how I was going to prolong my conversation with Betty. I would have to come up with it as we went along. But she made it easy for me.

"She's not been home, either?" Betty sighed, holding the door open to direct me into her kitchen. "Your parents must be sick. Annie's been out the night, too, again, and doesn't care if I sleep a wink or not."

I stepped in with my mind churning. Part of me wanted to say, No, I was lying, Katie's home eating toast—don't think my sister is like your daughter. But another part of my brain was absorbing the information: Annie Peckford was out all night, and is out all night often.

"Why don't you wait here a while and see if the two of them honour us with an appearance?" Betty suggested. I nodded, and she brightened a little. "We can do some courting here in the kitchen, you and I, my son."

My son had the sound of another place in it, strange to me. When I heard it, I thought of Mr. Babcock remarking that Betty and her former husband had come from far away. But then I suppose that was true of everybody in West Spirit Lake, except for the Indian families in the four-room shacks on Tecumseh Drive.

Betty had already brewed tea in a brown pot. She now poured me a cup without asking if I wanted any, and politely pushed over the sugar bowl and a half-pint can of Carnation. I had never drunk tea before and wasn't sure how I might like it fixed, so I decided to try that first cup clear. (That's how I have taken it ever since.) Betty dumped so much of the evaporated milk and sugar into hers that the syrup she stirred up was whiter than the best of her teeth.

She slurped the top half-inch off her cup, then pronounced, "What will we do with those girls?"

I was stuck with the story that Katie was not sitting at home in our sunlit dining room, but, like Annie, waking up only then in some place with the curtains closed. "I'm just supposed to see if I can find my sister and bring her home," I said.

"They always come home," Betty said. "Until they don't."

"Where do you think they are?" I asked.

"Where doesn't matter much," Betty said. "It's who they're with."

So I asked, "Do you have any idea?"

At that Betty smiled a little. "Would you go after the brutes for me if I named names?" she said. "Fight for your Katie's honour and my Annie's in the bargain? My love. If only you had come around just to sweet-talk me."

This was the old stuff between us, the marina banter, and I started to forget I was telling untruths over tea in a strange house. I was getting more used to the bitterness with every sip. And the unfamiliarity of Betty's kitchen—the clutter of cans and cartons that my mother would never have permitted—was growing to seem not so bad. It didn't appear dirty. The only out-of-the-ordinary smell was the muskiness from a stained blanket on the linoleum beside the table, Curly's bed.

So I sat back and ventured something more than a question. "If they were in town with some boys, I think one of us would know about it. I hear what kids say at school; you hear stuff at the marina."

"They're not in town exactly," she said. "It's the Blue Heron, where Annie serves tables. There's young men that pass through the place. Diamond drillers taking rooms by the week. Highway crews that stay a season. And a good-looking bartender or two, I'm told, not mention the cooks in the kitchen. Who's to say? But it's the Blue Heron, that much I know."

Nothing about the sergeant. Maybe I had more information than Betty. She took my silence for worry as I tried some more of my tea.

"Don't you fret overmuch about your big sister," she comforted me. "She's a good girl. I know—I was once one myself. Maybe still am. Don't laugh. You know, my son, sometimes things just happen to you. Sometimes you do things to yourself, sure. But other times things happen to you."

And how do we know the difference between what people do to themselves and what's done to them? That wasn't a question I could hear myself putting to Betty. My cup was empty. And, of course, I knew there was no chance of Katie showing up there with Annie. Yet I wasn't ready to let this talk end. When would I have another chance? I breathed in and made myself try something else.

"Betty, you know the new sergeant, Sgt. Martin? He lives out at the Blue Heron. I wonder why he doesn't step in if, like you say, the girls are staying out at the motel overnight or something?"

"That one," Betty said. "The way he whistles through his teeth . . ."

"What do you make of his whistling?" I asked too quickly.

Betty looked sharply at me. This was not the way to proceed. "It's nothing like an old-time piano waltz, I'll tell you that much," she laughed. "Nothing that I'd care to dance to, anyway."

What Betty made of what she heard was not something she revealed casually. I had gathered that much from Mr. Babcock, and should have known not to rush her.

That seemed to mark the end of our talk. I had not taken my boots off or even my coat, so I had only to stand up to leave. That seemed too hurried. Betty made it less abrupt by stepping out onto her back porch to see me off. Curly was lying down again, but stood up now for a pat on his back.

"Not much of a watchdog, is he?" Betty said with a laugh. "Letting a strange man stomp right up to my door. You might have come to rob me or worse."

Curly was poking his nose into my thigh. I gave him a tentative rub behind the ears, and said, "Good dog."

"He is a good dog," Betty chimed in. "Do you know he's fourteen years old? Nobody would guess it. Only thing my husband left behind that he ever wanted back. The bastard phoned me from the road somewhere the first night gone and said, 'You keep the kids, but I'll pick up Curly when I'm back your way.' I told him, 'The hell you will.'"

The recollection of that exchange caused a dry *ha*, *ha*, *ha* to rise up from her throat and swirl around in her mouth. Steel wool on the inside of a pot. I glanced around, worried that the inhuman sound would attract attention, and I'd be marked by some busybody standing at an odd hour on Betty's back stairs. But none of the neighbours were about. She went on.

"I'll tell you when I decided I'd never part with this animal. When my Annie was little, barely three years of age, she came inside from playing in the snow in this very yard with her brother (you've not met him and I trust you never will). Now, that was a cold winter, but Annie loved the out-of-doors. She sat down in her snowy things on my kitchen floor and tugged off her little boots, and her socks came off with them. In a blink, Curly is over to her, wagging, still a pup really, and he licks little Annie's bare toes, and then takes her wee foot in his mouth whole, but careful, like a good retriever with a dead duck.

"I'm thinking, 'What's this now?' And I says, 'Leave off, Curly, you crazy hound,' and I give him a little kick away with my slipper. But back he comes, whimpering a bit, and goddamned if he doesn't put his doggy mouth over that little baby's foot again.

Annie doesn't seem to mind, but I'm thinking, 'What's got into this canine?' So I kick him away again, but now I takes a good look at Annie's little toes. And they're white, you see, white. I can tell it's frostbite. I never felt worse. Doctor said we were lucky none fell off."

We stood together for a short time, petting the dog. Then I walked to the back gate and out into the alley as Betty turned inside and Curly lay down again on the concrete.

I crunched along, thinking about things that had nothing to do with the sergeant, the safe, and my sister. I remembered once being told that the roof of a well-bred dog's mouth was black, and the gums, too. Only the tongue should be pink. Curly's mouth, I had noticed, was all pink. But then nobody paid much attention to signs of a dog's pedigree in West Spirit Lake. The colour of the inside of a dog's mouth was as much a mystery as the qualities that might make it try to warm a toddler's frozen toes, or catch frogs just to let them go.

I thought also about Betty Peckford's son, Annie's brother, in prison. The boy who had been playing with his little sister the day she froze her toes. Where was he when Curly had tried to warm them? Betty hadn't put him in the story. Did he sit in the waiting room at the hospital, worrying that maybe he, the older one, was to blame?

I walked to the arena where I found Julius and Mike nearly done flooding the ice for the day's games. They were working without talking. Ever since the discovery of the safe, Julius mostly brushed aside attempts at conversation. He showed no sign of wanting us to leave him alone, exactly, but it was clear he was unwilling to talk. As Julius drove his little tractor off the ice surface, I helped Mike coil the heavy hoses and hang them on the wall beneath the stands.

"I've been talking to Betty Peckford," I started.

"What else is new?" Mike scoffed. "You're always at it with that old bat."

"No, this is different," I said. "I got her to tell me Annie is out all night all the time out at the motel."

"So? That's what I've been telling you," he said. "She's screwing the sergeant."

"It looks that way," I said. "What's it got to do with the safe, though?"

"Fuck all, probably. Unless Annie's in on the gold."

"You're so sure it's high-grading," I said. "It could be something else."

"It's gold," Mike said with absolute certainty. "Get this. My old man was happy drunk last night. Payday. After I let him beat me arm wrestling, I said, 'Hey, Dad, why don't you cut yourself an extra bonus and bring home some high-grade some day?' And he gets all serious and says, 'Hey, I'm no goddamn high-grader, I'm a miner.' But then he says, 'Anyway, you little shit, what am I going to do with this gold, make your mama some earrings?'"

Mike was doing a good impersonation of his father, adopting at the same time a French accent and the way a drinking man separates his words. He went on: "So I said to him, 'I'd sell it, that's what.' And he laughs at me, 'To who? To who are you going to sell? You need a middleman for that, a smart guy who won't get caught. Who's smart like that in West Spirit?'"

Mike let his father's astute question hang in the unmoving air of the empty arena. We were down in the dark corridor where Julius coiled his hoses and hung them on the wall. Of course, we both had the same answer in our minds: the new sergeant was a smart man. We went into the little room where Julius was sitting, eating his peculiar breakfast of yogourt and chopped onion and cold sausage. He looked up at us and away. His red metal tool chest had been rolled into its spot under the table again, but we all knew the safe was tucked behind it.

"Julius," I said. "Mike and me think maybe you should tell whoever left that strongbox here to put it somewhere else."

Julius kept chewing and swallowing. Then he drained his coffee cup and wiped the inside carefully with his handkerchief, a rag really, which he kept tucked in the back pocket of his coveralls. He picked himself up and lifted his heavy coat down off a nail beside the door and walked out of the little room. Mike and I followed him, a few paces behind. I was unsure if I should say anything else. I felt I had made a mistake.

"You think about it, Julius," Mike pleaded in a way that was strange for him, his voice rising a few notes higher than usual, letting me hear how he must have sounded when he was a little kid, before he moved to our town. "You know, do what you have to do. You don't have to listen to us."

Then Julius drove off in his truck to his island and he did not come back across the lake again that season to make perfect ice at the West Spirit Lake Municipal Arena.

CHAPTER 10/

As a boy I knew that I could impress adults. I didn't show off, not blatantly, but made my presence felt. Katie played piano and brought home perfect pictures she had drawn in school; my talents were not so apparent. I could ask an interesting question and put on a face that showed I was listening hard to the answer. One time our family friend, Mr. Brascomb, was holding forth over supper about the attractions of certain places he had visited—the cobbled streets of Quebec, the Everglades of Florida. "Mr. Brascomb," I asked, "why do some people travel and other people like where they are?" I might have been eight when I put this to him. I enjoyed the pause as he thought about how to answer me.

Then there was a sort of game I played with my mother that we both enjoyed. If she had something on her mind—and I could usually tell—I would make myself available for her to talk about it. I might hang around the kitchen while she dawdled clearing the table, or linger in the living room as she looked out the window, smoking with one hand, holding a magazine folded open in the other. After a while, she would start to speak, as if without thinking. "Your Grandma sounded so old to me on the phone last Sunday . . ." or "Your father looks so tired these days. . . ." I would take it all in without saying much, until she would look at me as if just realizing I was there, and say, "Now, this is silly, talking like this—you're just a little mouse." I have never felt more myself than in those moments.

By the winter when I was thirteen, though, time was running out on these ways I had. What's fine for a kid can seem sly in an adolescent, and I began to sense this. I was no longer so easy about nosing into the adult world, even though I was coming closer to joining it. Yet that March I needed more than ever to find out things that I believed only men and women might tell me. The tug in the other direction I was feeling—an urge to curl back into childhood until grown-up life claimed me for good—wouldn't take me anywhere.

On the third morning in a row that Julius failed to show up at the arena, the town office sent someone to White Dog Island to check on him. The lake ice remained solid, with spring breakup still a few weeks away, so it wasn't time yet for his regular week or two of forced solitude on the island. That would come when the ice turned rotten.

Besides, the hockey playoffs were just starting, the most antic-ipated games of the season, and Julius was needed more than ever to do his work. I never learned exactly what he told the town's emissary, but somebody at the municipal office called my father and asked him to put together a package of over-the-counter cold remedies to send over to the island. It was all anyone could think to do since the old man refused to see a doctor. "Any idea what's ailing your friend Julius?" Dad asked me that evening. "It's not healthy for an elderly man like him to hole up like this." I shrugged and heard myself fibbing that I thought maybe I had heard Julius coughing a little or sniffling.

Mike and I were called to the office the following afternoon. It was no shock that along with Mr. Kenison, Sgt. Martin was waiting there. As the town's most winning hockey coach in mem-ory, the sergeant had a direct stake in making sure the arena had reliable ice. He was leaning against the front of Mr. Kenison's old wooden desk, positioned so that our principal, seated in his swivel chair behind it, had to crane his neck to get a look at us around Sgt. Martin's uniformed figure.

I didn't care much about Mr. Kenison, but I was annoyed by how the sergeant was blocking his view. There was plenty of room for him to stand someplace else.

"Looks like we need you two to make ice again for a while," the sergeant started off. "Julius is out of commission."

"You'll never know the difference," Mike assured him. "We're your guys."

"You'll have to do," Sgt. Martin said. "Any idea what Julius might have come down with? He doesn't seem to have a lot of time for the medical profession."

"He had a pretty bad cold last weekend," I lied.

"Did he?" said the sergeant. "And how about you? How's your chest?"

I wanted to look away but made myself keep staring into his light blue eyes, which were now fixed on me. The office smelled of dust and dry glue from the spines of cheaply bound books. "My mom and dad don't want me to go back to hockey yet," I said. "But I'm allowed to help out with the icemaking a bit."

"Too bad you won't be lacing 'em up again," he said, but he didn't sound sorry. "The team's on track for a championship. Aren't we, Mikey?"

"It's in the bag," Mike said.

During this exchange, I took four steps over to the side of the office so that Mr. Kenison could see me without having to look around the sergeant. This forced the sergeant to make a half-turn to keep me in his line of sight, and prevented him from leaning so comfortably on the edge of the desk. He shifted his weight, crossed his legs, then uncrossed them again, and finally stood erect.

For the rest of the discussion he loomed over us, but I forced myself to fix my attention mostly on the principal, deferring to him, even when the sergeant was speaking. Mr. Kenison kept looking down at the papers on his desk, giving me every chance to turn my gaze back to the sergeant. But I wouldn't.

The arrangement would be much the same as during freeze-up back in the fall. Until Julius returned to the job, Mike and I would be excused from school early every weekday to go make ice. On weekends, we'd be expected to arrive at the arena first thing. Our parents would be called to make sure they agreed, but we already knew they would. Then Sgt. Martin left the principal's office with us.

In the hallway, he put one hand on Mike's shoulder and the other on mine. As we walked slowly back to class, I looked at the red stripe that ran down the outside seam of his pants.

"Anything bothering Julius that you guys could tell me about?" he asked, lowering his voice to complete the circuit that his hands had begun. "Between us, I'm worried about the old guy."

There was a silence then that I knew we shouldn't let last long, but I couldn't bring myself to break. I could think of nothing but the humid heat of his hand through the cloth of my shirt. Mike saved us.

"Bothering Julius?" Mike said. "How the hell would anybody know? Half-nuts old bohunk, talking to himself and everything all the time."

"Watch your language, St. Vincent," Sgt. Martin said, his voice back to normal. "This is a school, not a pinball arcade."

A half-hour before class would be finished for everybody else that day, Mike and I were freed to head over to the arena. All that afternoon I had been distracted by the idea that I could almost hear Mike's thoughts, as if a string ran between our brains like two tin-can telephones. And I imagined he was straining to make out what I was thinking, too.

But once we were out on the street, we didn't have much to say to one another.

After we had walked a few minutes, I asked, "What do we do now?"

"We make ice," Mike said.

"You think the sergeant knows how much we know?" I asked. "About the safe, I mean."

"He's got to figure maybe the safe is why Julius isn't coming to work," Mike said.

"We need to tell somebody," I said. "Maybe the old sergeant."

"We don't tell anybody a fucking thing," Mike said. "Why is it our business anyway? So he's high-grading some gold off the company and getting his jollies with some waitress. Who gives a shit?"

When Mike talked that way I couldn't match him. It was the way they spoke around the rec hall pool tables, I guessed, or maybe the way his father did while drinking beer and arm wrestling at their kitchen table. But it wasn't just the way Mike was talking that shut me up. He had a point. It was true that I wasn't sure what any of it had to do with us. I wasn't even certain why I was going to the arena with Mike that afternoon. I only knew that I needed to know more, to get the sort of information that could come only from an adult. And the only adult I could think of turning to just then was old Julius.

"Can you flood the ice on your own?" I said. "I'm going to see if I can get Julius to tell us anything."

"You're going to walk across to the island now?" Mike said. "It's daylight, somebody will see you."

"I'll stop at my dad's drugstore and pick up some cough candies or something to take over to him. What's anybody going to think?"

So that's what I did. I ran to the pharmacy and asked my father for a package of cherry lozenges. He asked me to wait until quitting time and he'd drive me over to the island. But I said no, it was mild enough out, and I didn't mind walking. He let me do what I wanted, the way he almost always did.

The snow on the lake ice had crusted over with the freeze and thaw of warmer days but still frigid nights. Walking on it was slow going; my boots broke through the crust every second step, putting me up to my knees in grainy snow. The only way to make headway was to slide along in one of the ruts Julius's truck tires had worn driving back and forth on the same route just about every day of the winter. These ruts went right down to black ice. I stopped and stared at this surface as if there were a chance of making out the movement of water or even fish far below. I knew better—the ice was several feet thick and opaque as marble—but I couldn't resist taking a long look.

Sliding along in one of the ruts, it took me fifteen minutes to make the half-mile to the island. I saw that Julius's snow-covered dock had been wrenched out of line by the ice, and would have to be straightened and levelled in the spring. There was an oblong hump in the snow where he had pulled his little boat up on shore and turned it upside down for the season. His pickup was parked just beside it, and a pathway up to the cabin was neatly shovelled. The walk was covered with fresh sawdust and wood chips that Julius must have collected for just this purpose when he sawed and split logs for heat and cooking.

He had seen me coming. From his two windows facing the lake, there would be no missing a lone figure crossing the ice. So he opened the door before I had a chance to knock. "Not windy today," he said, holding it for me. "Nice for walking."

I came in and let my eyes adjust. I had never been in Julius's cabin before. But it was exactly the sort of place I had often imagined, although I might have hung a rifle over the mantle. One main open room extended across the entire front of the cabin, no more than twenty-five feet across. The stone fireplace at the far end was not lit, but the black stove in the kitchen was throwing lots of heat. The one bedroom in the back was off the kitchen. Julius's books, maybe two dozen in all, were on shelves within easy reach of the kitchen table; I recognized the covers of some from when he brought them to his little room at the arena. The table itself was covered in oilcloth that was decorated with fading stripes and flowers. The only thing on it now was a black transistor radio, quite new.

I pulled the package of cough drops out of a plastic bag and also a newspaper that my father had suggested I bring. "From my dad's store," I said. Julius nodded and moved his lips in what I took to be a thank you. He sat down on a wooden kitchen chair and pushed the one across from it out from the table with his foot. So I sat, too.

I asked, "How are you doing, Julius?"

"How am I doing. Very good."

I wasn't sure if he meant to say he was well or was commenting on my question.

"Everybody thinks you're sick or something," I went on. "I don't know what to tell them."

"Why must you tell them?" he asked.

"They think Mike and me know; we're your helpers, right?"

Julius laughed at this in a way I had never heard from him. It was not a little chuckle that might be followed by his mumbled *goody-goody*. This was a partly choked-back laugh that came out unwillingly enough to make him shake slightly, a tremor that went through the kitchen table to me. I realized how small a man he was. He was wiry, but at that moment, I saw clearly how, in not too many years, he would be frail.

"Julius, we know you're not sick. What we want to know, Mike and me, is why is that safe in your room at the arena. I mean, maybe we're wrong, but we don't think it's so good to have it there."

The way he peered at me as I made this little speech, he didn't look like a funny old guy. He was a thinker. At the arena, he was always doing something with his hands—working on his icemaking equipment, or at least sipping tea and turning the pages of one of his old books. Now they looked so still, his two mottled hands and his bare forearms, lying flat on the oilcloth in front of him. Only his mind was busy.

Finally, he asked, "Do you know where the old man comes from?"

"Europe," I said. "Latvia."

"Good. Smart boy listens," he said. "I was a smart boy, too. Do you know what I liked when I was a smart boy? Soldiers. And trains." He looked at me for a few seconds. "But you don't know these things."

It was true that I had never seen a soldier in real life and the nearest train tracks intersected the highway a full two hours' drive south of West Spirit Lake, at a mill town where fresh lumber could be seen piled up,waiting to be stacked on freight cars. There were no train whistles in my boyhood.

"When I got a little older," Julius went on, "I didn't anymore like these things so much, soldiers and trains. Too many trains full of soldiers and people going where they don't like to go."

He thought for a minute, closely examining his own hands and arms, motionless before him. Then he added, "And the authorities," as if these words flowed somehow from what he had just said.

"When I came to Canada, I thought there were no authorities here. But everywhere there are authorities," he said. "Before this island, I had a long life. But my wife dies, my daughter marries. She moves away. I say, here, take money. Why does the old man need money? Take. Very good. I'm a little crazy. I think, why should I pay this bank now? Why should I pay this telephone? Why should I open this envelope and this envelope and this envelope? I think, the old man is not opening anymore. The old man is not paying anymore."

Again, Julius took time to breathe. Now he drummed his fingers one at a time very slowly on the table, as if he were testing them each in turn. They were straight at the joints and brown and brittle-looking.

"But you have to pay. Listen to the old man. After a few months, police come. Julius, you must open envelopes. Julius, do you have money? What about insurance? What about your bank? Everything to my daughter, I say, she thinks I have a big pension. Then one policeman says, Julius, you should go away from this town.

"This policeman," Julius looked up from his fingers and straight into my eyes, "this policeman knows what it is to be alone. He knows also a place to go live for not much money, only a little up the highway. You go, he says, leave your envelopes behind. Everybody will forget. He tells me about a little cabin"— here Julius lifted up his hands from the table to take in his home—"empty, not expensive, not so far away."

I wondered if he really had to run. But Julius was a man who listened to the authorities. And, of course, I knew the identity of the police officer whose plan for escape Julius had followed to White Dog Island.

"That's why you have to keep the safe?" I asked.

Julius was again looking at his hands on the patterned oilcloth, palms now toward the low ceiling. He rapped his silver wedding band, click-click-click, and bobbed his chin in time, yes, yes, yes. I didn't know how to judge the decision he had made. Was he acting out of a sense of gratitude to Sgt. Martin, or fear that a few unpaid bills he had run away from years before might yet somehow catch up with him?

"Do you know what's in it?" I asked.

He raised his eyebrows and tipped his head to one side in a way that reminded me of a robin hunting worms. "Why does a smart boy want to know this? Concerning the authorities, better to not know. Listen to the old man. About what goes in a strong-box, there is only one thing—money."

No, I thought, gold, too. I stood to leave. Julius turned in his chair and squinted out his kitchen window. "Lots of light still for walking," he said, then added with a thin, conspiratorial smile, "The old man is too sick to drive you home tonight. Sorry. Thanks to your father for candies and newspaper."

So I trudged back across the ice as the sun set behind me. The edge of the sky was ballpoint blue behind an even darker, jaggedly serrated horizon line of Jack pines and black spruce. Higher overhead the sky was streaked with flesh colour. The earliest crescent moon, barely a fingernail, poked through, along with the puncture points of the first few stars. Even with the daylight draining away, it wasn't all that cold. Windless.

As I walked along in the narrow ruts worn by the right-side tires of Julius's truck on his way out to the mainland, the left-side ones on his way home, I saw how the darkened windows of our house, and all the other windows of West Spirit that faced out over the lake, reflected the same rectangular patch of the sky. They were as identical as postage stamps. I couldn't make out anyone watching through them, but I felt eyes on me.

It turned out I was right. When I got home, Katie was waiting. She hustled me into her room, something she had never done before, and closed the door behind us.

"What were you doing over on the island?" she demanded.

"Taking Julius some stuff from Dad."

"You're a little angel of mercy."

"What's the matter with you?"

"You're nosing into stuff you don't know about," Katie said in a husky whisper that scared me. "Leave it. You and your little friend, leave it."

"What friend? What are you talking about?"

"Don't try your little-boy game on me. I see you. I see you." Then dropping to an even darker whisper, she went on, "I'm talking about the thing at the arena. I'm talking about your little spy friend, Mikey."

That was what the sergeant had taken to calling him.

"Mike and me know what's going on," I said, my voice breaking a little. "You'd better get out of it, Katie. It's all going to end. I talked to Julius and tomorrow I'm going to talk to the old sergeant."

I was making the decision about my next move as I spoke the words.

We had been facing each other in the middle of Katie's room, standing close. Her breath was sweet. What would it smell like with beer on it? Mom had recently put a small rug beside Katie's bed, one she ordered from a catalogue, which fit her notion of a teenaged girl's taste. It was shaggy and had a big pattern of orange and brown squares. Now Katie sat down on her bed, and I was left standing alone on the new rug. There was a certain stiff feel to it on the toes, even through socks, like coarse animal hair.

Katie looked at me as if she didn't know me and grew quieter. "What do you have to tell the old sergeant about?" she asked, and then quickly corrected herself. "What do you *think* you have?"

"About the gold."

She nodded her head slowly, exactly the way our father sometimes did when something puzzled him. "The gold," she said as if these were words from a foreign language. "The gold."

"You'd better get out of it," I said again. "Or tell Mom and Dad—I won't tell them. I'm going straight to the old sergeant."

"I'm not in it," she said. "Not like you think, you little sneaky moron. Do you understand me? You don't have anything to tell."

She spun to the wall and I left her room.

A half-hour later, I was amazed by how casual Katie was over dinner. She sat and ate as if everything were fine. She didn't look at me much, but she didn't make a show of keeping her face turned away from me, either. I was sure our parents were detecting nothing out of the ordinary in the air between us. Her voice was normal. My own sounded strange to me, but they didn't pick up on it.

When we finished eating, we all went to the living room to watch TV. In those days, there was only one channel available in a place like West Spirit Lake. So we watched the same shows as everybody else on our street, everybody else in our town. Sgt. Martin was probably watching in his room out at the Blue Heron, alone or with company, the pulp trucks droning past on the highway, their rear tires kicking up gravel from the shoulder on the corners. Betty would be watching in her little house, the St. Vincents in theirs.

But it occurred to me that I hadn't seen a TV in Julius's cabin. He was the exception, I guessed, listening to the radio at his kitchen table. The only other sound might be his own muttering as he read the newspaper I had brought him. And the fire in his stove, another murmur. And from outside the occasional deep groan—the lake ice adjusting to the milder nights, the easing of the sub-zero grip, shifting along the unseen, deep, fault lines, above which the first open water would show in only a few weeks at breakup time.

CHAPTER 11/

The day after I visited Julius was a day of deception. I awoke early from a bad sleep, not rested. I had made up my mind to go to the old sergeant, Sgt. Kowalchuk, first thing that morning and tell him everything I knew. I would not inform my parents first, and I wasn't going to let Mike in on what I was doing, either.

The decision was simple enough, but through the night, my plan became mixed up with dreams. In them, Sgt. Kowalchuk was never himself, and I did not always play the correct role. Sometimes Mike went to reveal the truth instead of me, and I only watched from a hidden place. Or if it was me who went to the police detachment to come clean, someone other than the old sergeant would be there to listen to my secrets. It was a woman, old or young, and then it was the new sergeant. Or another man, and I could never quite make him out. I slept and half-slept, woke up, slipped again into these variations many times.

When the light of the late winter morning made it impossible to find my way back into the dreams again, I lay for a long while, thinking over what I meant to do that day. I was in no rush to get up. If I stirred before my normal time, my mother might suspect something. And I didn't want to sit down for breakfast until my father had left for work, because he could often guess when something was on my mind.

But even after I had spent a long time awake, sorting through my dreams, I could still hear him talking with my mother in the kitchen. Usually he was quicker to get off to the store. Then, as I listened, I realized they were not having their usual morning chat. Their voices were different. And why had nobody turned on the radio? And where was Katie's voice? She was almost always up before me and usually took her time over breakfast.

I hopped out of bed quietly and slipped down the hall towards the kitchen. "At least she phoned," my mother was saying. "That's something."

"That's something?" Dad said, restraining his voice with effort, no doubt to keep from waking me. "You're giving her credit for checking in? Jesus Christ. She's seventeen. She sneaks out in the middle of the night and calls at, what, five in the morning, from Christ knows where, and you're giving her points up for phoning?"

"Think about it," Mom said. "Would she have phoned at all if she was up to anything so terrible? I heard her voice, dear, you didn't. She sounded upset, not guilty."

"Goddamn it," he said. "You're going to tell me her tone of voice makes all this just fine."

"I'm telling you to wait until we have a chance to talk to her."

Then they fell silent, so I came from the hallway into the kitchen. "Talk to who?" I said as casually as I could manage.

They looked at each other.

"Your sister," Mom said. "She was out a little late last night and stayed over at a friend's house."

"Whose house?" I asked.

"Never mind," Dad said.

I shrugged to suggest I didn't care and poured myself a bowl of cereal. Everything normal. Eat, dress, head out the door.

When I was outside, I had to remind myself to start running, the way I always did. My feet felt heavy and my head unclear. Down the street, up the path through the birch grove that separated the houses along the lakeshore from the main townsite up on its plateau. There was damp in the air and the snow was wet enough for snowballs. The black stripes against the white of the birch trunks were darker than they had been a few days ago, a sign that the bark was no longer stiff with frost, but growing moist.

Jogging out of the trees, I altered my usual route, turning away from the school. If anybody happened to notice me, they might wonder where I was going at that hour. But why would anyone give it more than a passing thought? The druggist's kid is always running somewhere. But there's not much out that way he's heading except the highway. Only the provincial police detachment, right on the edge of town, and then the Blue Heron Motor Hotel, a bit beyond. And, another mile or so farther, the airport, where they fly out the gold bricks once a week, without which this town of West Spirit Lake wouldn't be here at all.

I had visited the police detachment before, on school outings during traffic safety week. It was a single-storey, yellow-brick building, with two flagpoles out front and a garage big enough for six cruisers. Only the little jail had interested me and my friends much—two cells, mostly used for drunks to sober up in overnight. But I remembered the building from those class tours as a busy enough place, with cops in uniform coming and going, and a couple of secretaries typing out forms, all with staticky radio noise in the background.

Now the place seemed almost deserted.

I asked the officer sitting alone at the front desk if I could see the old sergeant.

"The old sergeant?" he asked. "What do you mean, the old sergeant?"

"I mean Sgt. Kowalchuk," I said. "Not the new sergeant."

"Not Sgt. Martin, you mean," he said. "You're sure as heck not going to see Sgt. Martin anytime soon. And not Sgt. Kowalchuk today. Is this a school fundraising thing?"

"No, it's important," I said.

"Important," he said. "There's a lot important going on. You'd better come back next week or something, okay?"

I'm just a kid to him, I thought. He doesn't know about anything. The safe. The party. My sister, my sister's secret friend. I turned toward the door, wondering what to do now. But as I hesitated to open it, the constable behind the counter called after me.

"Just a second," he said. "This important matter you have to talk to Sgt. Kowalchuk about, it doesn't have anything to do with what's going on out at the Blue Heron, does it?"

"I don't think so," I said.

"Just checking," he said. "You have your teacher call and make an appointment next week when things quiet down—"

I was outside before he finished. I saw now that there was only one police cruiser parked there, instead of the usual three or four. Where were the rest of them? I began running, or my legs did, away from town. My boots churned into the soft gravel shoulder of the highway—it had been firmer when I ran on it in the middle of winter. After a while, I adjusted my pace; there was no way I could keep up that speed all the way to the motel. As I ran, two cars passed me, also leaving West Spirit Lake behind. Both times as they went by I half-turned and stuck out my thumb, still running, but neither even slowed down.

Five police cruisers were pulled up at odd angles under the Blue Heron sign. An ambulance was there, too, but two paramedics were leaning against its hood, lazily sipping coffee from takeout cups: there was no rush to get anybody to the hospital. Three police officers were hovering around the doorway of what I knew was Sgt. Martin's room. The blind was drawn on the window that I had stared into that night to see my own sister looking out.

I had enough sense not to try walking straight into the lobby, or entering through the coffee shop, or by the double doors under the neon sign of the Wading Bird Lounge. I trotted around back, panting from my run. I had never had any reason to go back behind the motel before. Two men in white aprons, cooks or dishwashers, stood smoking and talking in low voices in the sunlight a few feet away from a row of trash cans and a pile of green garbage bags. On the motel roof, two ravens waited patiently for the men to go inside.

I couldn't think of a way to slip in without being seen so I simply walked up to the door in plain sight. The kitchen men didn't seem to care. They barely glanced at me. It was something Mike might have pulled off. I felt invisible. The kitchen was neater and cleaner than I would have imagined, but then breakfast must have been cancelled that morning. I glanced out the pass-through window and saw that the coffee shop was dark and deserted. Then I peered through the round windows of the swinging doors into the bar. Two more cops and a few motel workers, maids and waitresses, were clustered in two booths drinking coffee. Just apart from them, a woman was sitting alone at a table, her back to me.

It took me a few seconds to realize I was looking at Katie. Her hair reached just to below her shoulders, quite straight. But I remembered how curly it had been when we were little, and knew that it still went wavy if she came out of the water from swimming and let it alone to dry in the sun and a summer breeze. I pushed slowly through one swinging door and held it carefully with one hand to let it close gently behind me. Then I took a half-stride into the lounge and paused, still looking at Katie, still invisible to strangers. Finally she turned around, a statue coming to life. It was like the night when she was in Sgt. Martin's room and I was outside, except this time she saw me.

She was not exactly calm. Her face was frozen. The stiff sideways motion she made with her head—she might have been getting a stray wisp of her bangs out of her eyes—was toward the bathrooms. I let her go first, and then I followed. Nobody turned and noticed me walking along the wall. I kept thinking, you can't see me, you can't see me.

"What are you doing here?" Katie whispered, turning the lock on the ladies' room door after me. "How did you know I was here?"

"I didn't know," I said. "All I knew was something was going on out here."

"Do Mom and Dad know?" she whispered. "Are they on their way?"

"No. I don't think so, anyway," I answered. "What's going on?"

"Somebody's dead. The cops won't say who. I think it's my fault."

Tears started flowing down her face as she said this, even though she controlled her voice and her mouth was set. They streamed down evenly from both eyes, and droplets formed quickly on the line of her jawbone, and from there began to fall to the front of her shirt, one drop on one side, then an identical drop on the other.

"How's it your fault?" I asked. "You don't even know who it is."

"I told Annie last night," she said. "I told her you were going to tell the old sergeant about the safe. She said we had to come out here right away. Then, I don't know, we told Bobby. He's not as bad as you think. Nothing ever happened. And I went to wait in the lobby while they sorted stuff out. I waited all night."

"Sort what stuff out?" I asked. But she wasn't really listening.

"God," she said. "God. God. Something happened in his room."

What she had called Sgt. Martin a moment earlier made it hard for me to concentrate on anything else she was saying. I must have heard before then that his first name was Robert. But the name she used made it seem she was talking about a different person entirely, somebody I didn't know at all: Bobby. It sounded like some sort of bad joke, one I didn't quite get.

I heard myself asking, "How did you get out here in the middle of the night?"

"Betty's old car. It's out back."

I knew Betty's car very well, a Pontiac Superchief, black and not too badly rusted, with a red vinyl interior. Usually it was parked in her alleyway, rarely driven.

"It's not out back," I said. "I came in that way. There's no cars at all parked out there, nothing but garbage."

"Then somebody must have taken it," she said. Her mind was still working, even though the tears kept coming. "We parked it out back. Annie let us in with her waitress key."

"Then what?"

She wiped her eyes with her sleeve like a kid and went on. "Then we talked to him. Then Annie said she needed to talk to him alone," she said. "That wasn't any of my business, so I waited in the lobby. I guess I fell asleep there on the couch. The sirens woke me up, the cop cars and the ambulance." The tears were starting again, and this time her face was losing its perfect shape.

"I'm going to check out his room," I said.

"No," she said. "How?"

"I'm invisible."

There was nobody at the front desk. I walked straight past it to the long hallway that connected the lobby to the rooms. There were only ten of them. The sergeant's was the second-last one, number nine, that lucky number in hockey. When I was about halfway down the hall, two cops stepped out of the sergeant's door, talking in low voices with their chins down. The shorter one was Sgt. Kowalchuk. I felt I would not be invisible to him, so I squeezed into the alcove where the Coke machine hummed and glowed. There was an ice machine, too. I realized I was thirsty, and was tempted to reach in and take a cube to suck on.

When I couldn't hear the voices anymore, I poked my head out and saw that the hall was empty. I hustled the rest of the way to the sergeant's door, bringing my boots down softly on the carpet. Then I stood for a minute, listening just outside the room. There was no sound at all, so I went in.

At the foot of the two double beds was a gurney of stainless steel. On it was a body covered with a white sheet and belted into place. I took in every contour of that sheet in a glance. I've heard that most people look smaller dead, but that was not the case with Sgt. Martin under this shroud. His feet, which were closest to me, seemed huge. His barrel chest was enormous, a great hill.

His chin, even though it was exactly his under the clean cotton, jutted more prominently than it had in life.

I felt sick. To my left was the bathroom, but a strip of yellow tape had been placed at waist height across the door. I ducked under it. Inside, there was a lot of white debris, dust and chips of plaster, on the tile floor and scattered over the counter beside the sink. I saw that it came from where the ceiling over the tub had been smashed to expose wiring, plumbing, and a two-by-ten wooden beam. I leaned over the toilet, but I couldn't risk the noise of vomiting, so I gagged it down instead. What was bitter inside me would have to stay for a while, even though I was ready to be rid of it. Keeping it in made me very weak.

I stood breathing hard with my hands on my hips, and rolled my eyes up again. The cops had left dangling the strip of black leather that was tied around two copper pipes, I suppose because they meant to photograph it later. The leather had been cut neatly. The pipes had bent, but held.

I wanted to sit down, and I might have on the toilet or the edge of the tub, but I couldn't stand the thought of carrying that white dust out on my jeans. Why should I be marked by the evidence? I hadn't killed him. I wasn't even quite there. As I stood looking at the torn-up ceiling, my legs went wobbly, and an insane notion crossed my mind: go out into the room and lie down on one of the beds, the one that was still made, the one he had been stretched out on, leaning against the headboard, on that other night. Take a nap. Soon they would come in and wheel the sergeant out and not even see me. Then he'd be gone and I could sleep deeply.

I took command of my thoughts again, ducked under the tape across the bathroom threshold, and, without taking a backward look at the shape under the sheet, raced out into the hall. As I ran down it, I heard each muffled clump of my boots on the carpet separately. When I got to the far end of the hall, I could make out voices in the lobby. There was a door leading out to the back of the motel. I pushed through it, ignoring the Fire Exit Only sign.

The clanging of the bell and the sight of Katie waiting for me outside shocked me at exactly the same split second. She was standing where the cooks had been smoking when I passed them a half-hour earlier.

"Shit, shit, shit," she said, hearing the alarm go off.

We sprinted for the line of trees behind the motel, only about ten strides. We dived together into a thick tangle of bush just as two cops ran out through the door I had used.

As we flattened ourselves down into the wet snow, I whispered, "What are you doing here?"

"Shhh, you idiot," she said.

"Hey!" one of the cops shouted. "Who's out here! Come on out!"

But he was walking in the wrong direction, over toward the trash cans and the garbage bags. Maybe the movement of the ravens there had caught his eye. The birds seemed to know all the fuss had nothing to do with them, and continued tearing open green plastic. One had a chicken bone in his beak, and the other was looking for another like it. Both birds swivelled to keep an eye on the police, but they showed no sign of opening their wings.

"Whoever's out here, come on back inside now," shouted the cop. "Don't be stupid. Nobody's in trouble here. We just want to get everybody's statement, then you can go home. Day off."

We clung to the ground. I had my right cheek in the snow, which was icy and granular and studded with dead needles and twigs. Katie lay beside me with her left cheek down. After a few minutes the two cops gave up and went back inside, and I studied the hiding place we had found. The scraggly trees above us had grown tight together, and their lowest boughs dragged on the ground, weighed down by rotten snow. We were under that skirt. The bush around West Spirit Lake was mostly black spruce, but these were balsams. My father had taught me to recognize the flat needles and appreciate the healing smell.

I whispered again, "What are you doing here?"

"I didn't figure you'd go out the front way," Katie said. "And I didn't want to stay around to be interrogated. These dumb cops think I'm a coffee shop waitress or something, here for the morning shift. They don't know I came out with Annie last night."

"Annie's not in the room," I said.

"She's not in there?"

"No," I said. "Just the sergeant."

We were still lying side by side, our eyes and mouths not a foot apart. Her hair had caught a lot of needles and bits of bark and sticks. I didn't know how to go on and so I just looked at her.

"What?" she finally said. "What?"

"The sergeant's dead," I said. "He might have killed himself, I guess. He's on a stretcher thing. Under a sheet."

She closed her eyes tight and I suppose she was breathing in the medicine smell of balsam. I was absorbing it, too. I realized that the front of my pants and coat were soaking up melting snow, but I wasn't too cold. Might as well stay put until we were sure it was safe to move.

Whatever was happening while Katie kept her eyes shut was done by the time she opened them again. She was almost herself. She said, though not really to me, "Annie must have taken off in the car. Why didn't she come and tell me? She must have had to go fast. Why did he let her go like that? He let her go off and leave him behind alone in his room with me sleeping in the lobby."

She was getting it straight in her own head. I wanted to ask questions, but it didn't seem right to intrude. She was just putting the pieces together.

"We better go," I said after a time. "They're going to realize we're not in school. They'll call Mom and Dad and start looking for us."

We crawled out from under the trees on our elbows and knees, then ran over to the back of the motel kitchen, out of view of any windows. The ravens looked over at us where we stood pressed against the wall. They had a good feast spread out now. "Nice hairdo," I said to my sister.

"You, too," she said, and then, "Here, hold still," as she picked some balsam needles from my hair. It was like in the tree fort. I tried to get some out of hers, but I couldn't do much, her mane was so thick. When we got home, she would have to go carefully at it with a brush and comb.

We strolled out to the highway side by side. What else could we do? The paramedics by their ambulance looked up at us, but didn't see any reason to alert the cops, who were all concentrating on Sgt. Martin's room, not the open highway. We walked along on the shoulder and ignored the few cars that went by.

"Katie," I said. "Was Annie in on the gold?"

"The gold?" she said. "What gold?"

"In the safe," I said.

"Who told you that? Gold?" She didn't quite laugh. "No gold. Just Blue Heron money, from the cash registers. Bobby told Annie nobody would notice until they were long gone. They had a bartender in on it with them, Eric. Annie liked him. I wonder if he's gone with her now. I guess so."

No gold. I looked down, scuffling pebbles, as Katie sank back into her thoughts. She had an easier stride than me, much slower, and I would never have taken so long to get back to town on my own. As we walked along, what had just happened began to seem impossible, a variation on those bad dreams I had in the night.

Just as we were reaching town, we met our father driving out. We stopped walking. He did a quick u-turn on the highway, throwing up gravel on both sides, and came up beside us. I got in the back, taking the seat directly behind Dad so he couldn't easily turn around and look at me. Katie bravely took the front seat passenger side.

"You're soaked," he said. "Where have you been? No, don't answer me. Don't say a word. We'll talk about this at home. Your mother will want to hear this."

He drove with two hands on the wheel, rigid, staring straight ahead, as if he didn't trust himself to glance across at Katie or back at me. In only a couple of minutes we were home. There was a police car in the driveway. Normally, that would have been such a sight that my pulse would have raced, while all possible stories jostled for space in my thoughts, but now it was nothing. I knew that something was over and whatever was to come next would just be sorting things out.

CHAPTER 12/

The ice went out early that spring. Most years we didn't see much open water until around the middle of April. But in the first week of the month, two weeks after the death of the sergeant, a wind began blowing steady, straight up the channel that separated the town of West Spirit Lake from White Dog Island. It brought unseasonable heat from the prairies to the west, the combination of warmth and wear first stripping the snow off and then rotting the ice beneath, a little more every day. As always at breakup time, my mother could be found quite often with her coffee and cigarette by the dining room window, looking out over the lake.

I was hanging around home more than usual, staying indoors despite the sudden thaw. Since the morning at the Blue Heron Motor Hotel, nothing had been the same. For the first few days afterwards there were trips to the police detachment, several each for Katie and me, with Mom and Dad accompanying us into Sgt. Kowalchuk's office. We went often enough that I started to watch for things, such as the way the old sergeant slumped in his swivel chair, a posture that drew attention to his gut. We talked over the same details many times. When exactly did you say that safe showed up in Julius's little room? What do you remember, precisely, about seeing Sgt. Martin and Annie Peckford together?

I was a focus of interest around the schoolyard, as I suppose Katie must have been among her high school friends. Everybody heard how we had been out at the motel on the morning when the new sergeant's body was discovered. I was asked about it often. But the story was all over town within hours, and I soon realized that I understood no more about what had happened than anyone else.

Mike was interrogated as well, first by the police about the safe, and then by any kid who had the courage to approach him. From what I could gather, he said even less than I did. I believe his father had punished him for being involved in the affair at all, and I guessed severely. I tried to find out about it.

"Geez, my parents are pissed off about all this," I ventured to Mike one day. "How about your old man?"

"None of your fucking business," he said.

We were no longer on good terms. He was enraged over how I had acted without him, even though, as I tried to tell him, it turned out that I never got the chance to blow the whistle to Sgt. Kowalchuk. Everything that happened at the motel was set in motion before I said a word. "Like that makes it all just fucking fine," he said, stalking off toward his smoking place, where I was no longer welcome. And I knew he was right, that I had betrayed him. I had intended to break our bond over the knowledge of the safe, our suspicions about the new sergeant. That was what counted.

The safe was the subject of much speculation among adults trying to piece together the story. Some people seemed more intrigued by it than almost any other aspect of what had gone on. One afternoon only a few days after the sergeant died, I came upon Mr. Brascomb speaking about it to my father at the back of the drugstore. As I walked up, Mr. Brascomb fell silent, but Dad said, "No, Rick, go ahead. We're long past thinking we can keep this one in the dark about the whole matter."

So Mr. Brascomb picked up where he had left off, his eyes now flitting between my father and me. "Well, that safe is quite an item," he said. "It was the only thing that survived the fire that burned down the old Blue Heron Lodge way back when. It's a pretty thing, a real antique, you know, so they cleaned it up and kept it in the office of the motel all these years. A keepsake, you could say, of the old days."

He went on to muse about why the conspirators had stolen the safe when they began embezzling from the motel. They surely could have found a more discreet place to stash the money. Sgt. Martin's plan was simple enough. Annie Peckford was trusted most nights to close up the coffee shop; that bartender named Eric generally did the same at the Wading Bird Lounge. Part of their job was to count the register receipts, and then put the cash in the old safe overnight in the motel manager's office. Sgt. Martin persuaded them both to start skimming. It was inevitable that the owner would get suspicious, but the new sergeant said he would make sure he was assigned to the case, and then, of course, the investigation would never come to anything.

How much they hoped to steal, no one could say for sure. But around town everybody agreed it couldn't have amounted to more than a few thousand each. Hardly worth it. And then there was the safe. When it went missing from the motel office back in the winter, questions were asked. Who would want it? How had such a heavy thing been lugged out without anybody noticing? The motel owner figured somebody with keys to the office off the lobby must have taken it at night.

"It was taking the safe that did them in," Mr. Brascomb said. "It was what got Sgt. Kowalchuk poking around the motel. And that was what got Bobby Martin and the Peckford girl all panicky."

Now that the sergeant was dead, Mr. Brascomb was on a first-name basis with him.

"But why take the safe in the first place?" my father asked. "Why did they need the thing?"

"They didn't need it," Mr. Brascomb said. "That's the whole point. It was a matter of style. The new sergeant, he liked things looking good. Shined his shoes. Wore a nice overcoat. Had an eye for younger ladies. It's all part and parcel."

Then I heard myself saying, "Before hockey games, down in the dressing room, he used to comb his moustache in the mirror by the toilet."

This delighted Mr. Brascomb. The image of the new sergeant, shoes shined and coat immaculate, bothering to comb his policeman's moustache before taking his place behind the bench at a kids' hockey game became part of his portrait of the vain dead man. I was sorry to add this gem to Mr. Bascomb's string of telling details, and I resolved to be done with discussing the sergeant now that he was gone. I didn't quite keep that resolution.

Everything was over, and all wrapped up with such finality. Yet I felt less sure of what had happened and how I felt about it with each hour. It was like the way when winter ends you soon find you can't call up anymore the feeling of real cold. What below zero really means, its bite, never goes any deeper than skin. The knowledge of it soon melts away when the spring sun finds you.

I wanted to keep inside me something of what I had experienced, so I tried a few times to talk to Mike about it. On the morning after word went around that they had cancelled the hockey team's remaining playoff games, even though it was favoured to win, I approached him around the side of the school.

"They couldn't get anybody else to coach, I guess," I said.

"My old man would have," Mike said. "Nobody asked him."

"I guess mine might have, too," I said. "But maybe that wouldn't have been right. It was the sergeant's team. He was a great coach."

"Fuck you," Mike said. "You always hated him."

"I did not," I protested. "I tried to get along with him."

"Don't lie now he's dead," Mike said. "Don't fucking lie now."

He was getting a cigarette going as he said this and he coughed up smoke, something I had never seen him do before. He tried to take another drag and choked on it again, even more violently, this time the smoke leaking out of the corners of his mouth. "Goddamn," he said, rubbing his eyes with his fist.

"Shit." Something about watching him do this made my own eyes go wet. I wasn't sure what was happening, so I turned to walk off.

"You run have a good cry now, suckhole," Mike said. "Go cry with your big sister."

"Go to hell," I said, spinning around square to him, thinking, Let him see my face. "I saw him dead, you didn't. I saw where he did it."

"You must have been so fucking happy," Mike said. His face looked all messed up now, as if somebody strong had just slapped him. "What did he ever do to you? You hated him so much."

I'm not sure if I said, "I didn't, I didn't," loud enough for Mike to hear, or was lying only to myself as I walked away as fast as I could without breaking into a trot. Running would have been the worst thing now.

The next morning I told my mother I wasn't feeling well and asked if I could stay home. She didn't put a single question to me about my symptoms, just nodded with her lips pulled thin, somewhere between a smile and a frown. This expression brought out the tiny fans of wrinkles at the corners of her eyes, which reminded me of how pretty she was. In the two weeks since the sergeant died, she had never asked me a serious question about it all. Dad was the one who did the asking, and satisfied himself that I hadn't done anything seriously wrong. I almost wished they were angry with me, as they were with Katie for keeping Annie's secret, and whatever other confidences she hoarded.

That day when I got to stay home from school, my mother and I watched the start of a drama out behind our house. One good-sized tree stood there, a smooth-barked poplar of the sort that thrives up in that country. Most people preferred to plant white birch or blue spruce in their yards, and sometimes the fast-growing poplars were disparaged as weed trees. But my mother was fond of this one's rounded leaves, which she once told me looked to her like a handful of coins tossed up in the sunshine. The way she put it has always stayed with me, and I see every poplar that way still, when I think to look up at one.

So we liked our back-yard tree, and on that warm April morning, Mom noticed a pair of robins starting to build their nest in it.

"These two are getting an early start," she said. "They'll have time to raise two broods for sure this summer."

I looked out. One of the robins was laying a yellow blade of last year's grass on the beginnings of the nest. The other was singing on a high branch of the tree, up where the sap had just begun to reach and the buds were barely starting to show. "That'll be the male," my mother said, holding up her coffee cup in a toast to the singer. "The female is the one getting down to business—what else is new."

Off and on through that morning we kept watch on the robins. The nest took shape and Mom cranked open the dining room window a crack to catch the singing when we sat down together to eat canned soup and soda crackers for lunch. Then in the early afternoon, I heard her saying, "Well, well, who have we here." I came over to the window, where she was craning her neck to look up higher than the top of our poplar, into the clear sky.

"What?" I asked.

"Look," she answered.

The hawk was circling high, but not so high that there was any doubt about its identity. It was not a speck, like the bald eagle my father had drawn to my attention one summer morning when we were out fishing. This was a hawk shape. We watched without speaking as it drifted down, now out of sight above our roof, now back into view, a little lower than on the last circle, out over the lake.

"Go get the book," Mom said. "Not *Backyard Birds*. The *Water, Prey and Game Birds* one."

By the time I had fetched it, the hawk had landed in the low line of bush along the lakeshore at the bottom of our property. We would never have noticed its hunched figure there had my mother not followed the hawk all the way down from above. But knowing where to look, it was obvious enough, bulky in the scrub willows, too heavy for the slender branch that bent beneath it.

The robins knew it was there. The pair continued gathering

building materials, but they were distracted. The male dropped a strand of something grey on his way back to the half-finished nest.

Mom opened the book to the pages of hawks and falcons. "Can we make out our visitor's markings?" she asked. I stared hard at the hawk and saw the square corners of the tail, and something of the striped pattern of the feathers. I tapped one of the illustrations in the book. "Cooper's hawk," she read, looking first at the painting on the page, and then squinting at the shadow in the willow branches.

"That's our handsome fellow," she said.

I was taken off guard by her admiring tone. "Won't he go after the robins?" I asked.

"I don't think so," she said. "I think he'll be back after they lay their eggs."

"He wants the eggs?"

"He'll be looking for the chicks."

"No," I said. "I'm going out to chase him off."

"If you like," she said. "But we can't look out for these robins day and night, spring and summer. They'll have to guard their own nest, and we'll have to hope for the best. No use pretending otherwise."

So I didn't bother chasing off the hawk that afternoon. Later, a little before Dad and Katie came home, I looked outside again, and the threat was gone, at least for the time being. By then it was dusk, and Mom's interest had moved from the window to the piano. She was looking through the books of music that she taught her lessons from, playing little bits of tunes, and occasionally making a faint note in pencil to herself in the margins.

"Remember that rhyme about the robin you used to say to Katie and me when we were little?" I said to her. "'Who killed cock robin? I, said the sparrow, with my bow and arrow.'"

"Sure," she smiled. "You liked it and you didn't like it. 'Who'll dig his grave? I, said the Owl, with my spade and trowel, I'll dig his grave.' You'd pull your covers up when I got to that part. Remember the owl in the picture?"

"It seemed true that the owl would dig the grave," I said. "The part about the sparrow being the one that killed the robin, that seemed fake. What would a little sparrow have against a robin?"

"I wonder," she said, and turned again to the keyboard.

That one day home was as close as the death of the sergeant came to disrupting my life. I did my homework. I ran my errands. With the hockey playoffs cancelled for the sergeant's team, most of the boys my age had a lot of free time. And with the unusually warm weather, we all oiled up our bikes at least a month earlier than most years. Our weekly rides out to the airport to watch the gold being loaded on the plane resumed, but now we didn't talk so much about stealing it. That was a little kids' game. We talked about what we would do all summer, about girls, about turning fourteen, about going to high school in the fall. I started to have friends again.

Mike never came with us.

Katie went about her routine much as I went about mine. She didn't seem very affected by the fact that Annie didn't come home. Police picked up my sister's secret friend two weeks after she left the sergeant in his motel room. She was hitchhiking alone by the Trans-Canada outside Winnipeg. Eric the bartender had dumped her a few days before, and he was arrested not too many days later near Medicine Hat, Alberta. There was no courtroom in West Spirit Lake, so they were both tried in a bigger town to the south. Then Annie was sent still further south to some sort of reform school.

One day I asked Katie, "You heard when Annie is supposed to be coming back?"

"When do you think? Never," she said. "Ever."

Those rhyming words were the last she would ever say to me about anything to do with what had happened.

I guess *never* was on Betty's mind, too. The next time I saw her down at the marina, she had sunk deeper than ever into the old couch, and taken on more of its mottled colouring. I came in and she didn't even look up. Mrs. Babcock was carrying more of the conversation than I was used to hearing, with Betty only grunting or nodding, rarely putting three words together, and when she did, they came out as a little scuffling sound. You would have had to listen closely and lean in to catch what she was saying, and I had no real reason to care any more.

Julius stayed on his island as always through breakup time. I looked across now and then, and sometimes saw him chopping wood or puttering around his cabin. His dog bounced after him, or ran among the trees, her whiteness more visible from our side of the lake now that the ground was bare. By three weeks after the death of the sergeant, snow remained only in the shadiest places—pale patches where it was darkest—on the axis between two trees, say, where one threw its shadow in the morning and the other in the afternoon, or deep in the corner where two high walls met.

After seven days of warm, windy weather, I looked out on a Saturday morning to see that the lake was three-quarters open water. The ice held on only along the shore. I headed outside early to take a closer look.

The path took me toward Babcock's, but I didn't bother stopping there. I continued beyond the marina along the shore. The town quickly petered out, but the path stayed good for a half-mile or so. It led to a few docks and boathouses that had been built of scrap lumber where the shoreline curved in, not really forming a bay, just an indentation about as shallow as a tablespoon. Not much protection from the wind, but what was left of the ice could find no better place than here to gather to melt. The largest pieces were big enough to park a car on, but most were no bigger than a queen-sized bed. They were not packed in so tightly that glimmering seams of water couldn't be made out between them.

I walked to the end of the first dock I came to and jumped out onto the floe, something I had never done before. The ice moved beneath my boots, but not so much that I was afraid. It was solid, still a good six inches deep. Once I'd recovered my balance, I put one foot in front of the other, gingerly, until I reached the edge and could step, with just a little bounce, across the foot or so of water that was all that separated my first ice raft from the next one. And this was how I made my way out toward the morning-sky blue of the open channel.

When I was about as far from shore as I dared go, a voice called out to me, "You trying to drown yourself or just don't have any goddamn sense?"

It was Mike. He was standing on the end of the little dock with one hand held up to shield his eyes from the glare of the sun off the ice and water as he looked out toward me.

I turned to face him and widened my stance. Shifting my weight back and forth from one foot to another, I made the slab of ice I was standing on begin to rock. Soon the water started splashing up first on one side, then the other, and I had to put my hands out from my sides to keep balanced, but I kept on rocking.

He flung up his arms now and said, "You goddamn fucking lunatic!" Then he turned and paced away from me along the narrow dock, shaking his head as if he had seen enough and was leaving. But just as it looked as if he meant to step off the dock and back onto dry land, he pivoted, sprinted the length of the dock, and launched himself. As he hung suspended, his angled eyes round for once, and his mouth, too, I flew, and was there just beside him in mid-air. Then he landed on one foot, dead centre of the tabletop of ice he must have been aiming for, and I came back to my body, and watched him spring to the next slab without hesitating, then to the next, and the next, his compact body uncoiling as much as it needed to on every leap. This way he bounded as far from shore in twenty strides as I had picked my way in one hundred.

When he tried to stop on the ice raft next to mine, his momentum pushed him to its very edge, and he soaked one boot. "Holy shit, that's cold," he laughed. "I fucking near went in."

He sat down on the ice and took off the wet boot and the grey woollen sock beneath and wrung it out. Then he leaned back on his elbows and crossed his legs, holding his pink foot up in the sunlight, and draped the damp sock over his shin to dry out a little.

"I always said you were psycho," he said. "You do this every spring?"

I didn't want to say no, never once, so I just sat down on my own patch of ice as if I owned it, and gazed out toward open water in the same way Mike was. I closed my eyes and tilted my face into the sun. "I'm glad winter is over," I said.

"Goddamn right," Mike said. Then, in a quieter voice, "They finished with you down at the police detachment?"

"I guess," I said. "At least they haven't called for a week. You?"

"I'm done."

"Maybe they have it all figured out, then," I said.

"What's to figure?" Mike said. "They were ripping off the motel and when it looked like they were going to get caught, the crazy sergeant killed himself."

"You think he'd kill himself over maybe being caught with the money?"

"Who knows?" Mike said. "Looks that way."

"They say he tried this sort of stuff before," I offered. "Maybe this was one time too many." And I repeated one version of this piece of gossip that I had heard Mr. Brascomb tell my father— that Sgt. Martin had been pulled out of his last police post when rumours about money and girls started going around.

"Everybody knows that," Mike said. "They sent him here. Cops always give cops another chance."

Out of the corner of my eye I could see he had turned to study my profile across the few inches of open water that separated us. "But tell me this," he said. "Why didn't he just take off with Annie?"

"Maybe he thought they'd get caught anyway—"

He cut me off, saying, "So he thought he'd just string himself up instead? No way. There was some other reason."

I offered none. This mystery had already occurred to me and to all the rest of West Spirit Lake.

"Maybe Annie wasn't the one," Mike went on. I could feel that he was still looking at the side of my face, but I wouldn't turn to meet his eyes. "You know—not the one he was doing."

"You're the one who always said they were doing it."

"Maybe I was wrong," Mike said. "Who knows with all the

skanky girls in this town? Maybe it was somebody else he was doing it with."

Maybe it was somebody who said she wouldn't go with him, I thought, and maybe the sergeant decided he wouldn't go without her. Maybe he didn't kill himself because he was doing it. Maybe it was because he wasn't doing it. Maybe he wouldn't leave whoever she was. Maybe he was tired of running away from places all by himself. Maybe this was his way of staying.

"I guess we'll never know," I said.

Mike turned to face the sun again. "Who gives a damn anyway?"

Sitting that way, I could feel the seat of my pants getting wet from the ice melting a little underneath me. I unzipped my coat, tugged it off, and sat on it. So early in the spring the sun was not very hot, but it was just strong enough to take the edge off the breeze that I now felt through my shirt. I glanced over at Mike's ridiculous bare foot stuck out in the air, and he caught me looking and wiggled his toes. "Now this is fucking living," he said, and we both laughed.

Then he said, "I wish I had some smokes." Craving for something, Mike scratched at the ice a little with his fingernails and scooped what came loose up into his mouth.

I did the same. The surface was so weakened by the sun that when I scraped, it came away easily in little chunks of broken crystal. They wouldn't last long. The pieces caught the light as I held them in my palm before slipping a shard between my lips. And so Mike and I sat for quite a while, letting the meltwater trickle down our throats, not bothering to talk much anymore, eating the last of that season's ice in West Spirit Lake, and floating on it.